LIVES ENTWINED

ENCHAINED HEARTS, BOOK 1

EVE NEWTON

Lives Entwined
Enchained Hearts, Book 1

by Eve Newton

Copyright © Eve Newton, 2016, 2019

ONE

~Alex~

I'd been sitting at my desk for what seemed like forever. I loosened my tie slightly and went back to my project. I had put in more hours this month than anyone else and I couldn't see that changing anytime soon. The buzz of the main office died down to a hush that I still could hear from inside my office. My office that, while it had a window, over-looked the less attractive part of Manhattan.

I looked up from my laptop, curious as to the cause of the silence. And then I saw her. My mouth went dry and my heart thumped. Her cascade of raven hair fell in perfect waves over her shoulders. Her crisp, white suit showed off a figure that made me want to drool all over my keyboard. She was making her way to Angelo's office, the corner one I coveted but would probably never get, followed by her assistant and a couple more gawking employees. She disappeared from my view and, without getting up to stare out of my office at her, I let her image go.

She was a knockout.

She was the new boss.

Old man Bellingham had finally given up his office to his granddaughter last week and with only tiny glimpses of her in the past few days, no one except her assistant had been anywhere near her. And now she was here, on this floor. I was itching to get up out of my chair and hunt her down. I ached for just a glimpse of that gorgeous woman.

Man, I've got it bad. I shook my head. Not only was she the boss, she was so far out of my league, I might as well not even exist.

An angry shout shattered the silence. Something crashed in Angelo's office. The air was filled with expletives. Christ, he was not happy. I wondered what happened, but only briefly, because then I saw her again. She glided right past my glass-fronted office and my mouth dropped open. She looked at me with a slight tilt to her head, but she never stopped her confident stride. Her eyes were the color of emeralds and they glittered just as brightly, and then she was gone as quickly as she had come. I snapped my mouth closed as Rick sidled into my office and sat opposite of me with a self-satisfied look on his face.

"I know the deal," he said as he sat back and put his ankle to his knee.

I just looked at him, not giving him the satisfaction of asking. I was dying to know, but Rick was an arrogant son of a bitch who liked to think he knew it all. Encouraging him was not on my to-do list today. The silence grew in my office as the normal level of noise resumed on the floor, announcing the departure of *Lady* Bellingham. I glanced over Rick's shoulder. A door slammed and Angelo stormed to the elevators with a box in his hands. My eyes widened and found Rick's. He looked smug and then I had to ask, "What the fuck happened?"

"She fired Angelo!" Rick said with glee. "She went in there like butter wouldn't melt and canned his ass, effective immediately. She has balls, man, I'll tell you that."

"What?" I said in disbelief. "She fired him? Why?"

Well, actually I had an idea why. It was common knowledge that Angelo abused his expense privileges and that the Friday workday ended, for him at least, at lunchtime.

"Man," I shook my head.

"So, the junior V.P. spot is open," Rick said casually. "Amanda is already sprucing up my résumé."

I took that bit of information in just as casually. If that job was anybody's, it was *mine*. I put in more hours in a week than the whole lot of the other project managers combined. I wouldn't be overlooked for this. I knew I was a contender without having to spruce up my résumé, and a strong contender at that.

Rick changed the subject. "Drinks later?"

"Nah, too much to do," I replied, and Rick narrowed his eyes at me.

"One of these days you will have to loosen up. It's Friday, have a bit of fun." He stood and smoothed down his impeccable suit.

One day, but not today.

Rick left and I got back to work. My mind kept wandering back to the vision that was Ms. Bellingham. Several more cups of coffee later, I noticed the floor getting quiet again and realized it was time for everyone to go home. I wasn't going anywhere, though. This project was due on Monday and I wasn't jeopardizing a potential promotion by having it late or not up to scratch. I'd be here well after dark and likely all of tomorrow as well. I sighed and loosened my tie even more and then undid the top button.

AT TEN THIRTY, I called it a night, packed up my briefcase, and headed to the elevators while I checked my phone. Rick had been texting me for the last hour, telling me what a loser I was and what I was missing out on. I then got a visual of what I was missing out on and I snorted with mirth at the picture of my friend with a woman wrapped around him, practically drooling all over him. Yeah, Rick was a top-class prick, but he was also a friend.

The elevators dinged open and my breath caught in my throat as I looked up from my phone. There she was, standing in her crisp, white suit, looking like she had just put it on instead of being at the office for the last fifteen hours. She, too, was checking her phone and she looked up with a small frown as I stayed rooted to the spot. It deepened as I made no move to get in and as the doors started to slide shut, I jumped into motion. I jerked my briefcase up to force the doors back and I quickly stepped inside. I turned to face the doors and the ride down made me feel the most uncomfortable I had felt in ages. Her perfume consumed me. It was a heady scent, which made my dick go hard as I imagined inhaling it while I kissed her perfect lips and ran my hands through her luscious hair. I cleared my throat and turned my head to her.

"I'm Alex Monaghan," I said lamely.

She turned to me as she put her phone away. "I know," she said. "I'm Cassandra Bellingham."

"I know," I said, with what I hoped was a dazzling smile.

She laughed softly, her eyes sparkling, and my dick went on alert again. I moved my briefcase in front of me to hide the growing bulge in my pants. Oh God, she was gorgeous. Her eyes were like a cat's and her laugh was like molten chocolate and sweet honey all swirled in together.

"You're younger than I thought," I blurted out and then flushed bright red as her eyebrows went up.

"I get that a lot," she murmured and then her phone went off. She pulled it out and dismissed me.

I felt like the biggest jackass on the planet. I wanted to say something else to her, but the doors dinged open and she strode out of the elevator, leaving me to trail in her wake like a little puppy dog. This was fairly accurate though, as I probably looked like a dog with my tongue hanging out. She waved to the security team in the lobby and they all waved back with great enthusiasm. Joe raced to open the doors for her and wished her a good evening. She wished it back and his eyes followed her as she left the building.

I wanted to punch the old man in the face for looking at her but gave him a tight smile instead as I was left to open the door for myself, not important enough for Security to hold it for me. I watched her cross to a black Mercedes idling at the curb and the driver let her in. She caught my eye as she slid into the back seat. With a small smile, she vanished into the dark interior as the driver shut the door, cutting me off from my fantasy of sliding into the back seat with her and then *into* her as I lifted her skirt to have my way with her.

Oh fuck, I was sweating. I needed to get home, pronto. There was a single malt Scotch waiting with my name on it. Just the one, though, as I would be back at the office again tomorrow and I needed a clear head. I sighed and turned to head to the subway.

TWO

~Cassie~

I relaxed the second my ass hit the black leather seat of the Mercedes. This had been a bitch of a day. Actually, it had been a bitch of a week. I kicked my shoes off, leaned back and closed my eyes. Granddaddy had given me a whopper of a twenty-third birthday present last week. Not that I wasn't grateful; this is what I had wanted to do with my life, why my parents had spent vast fortunes on my overpriced education across the pond. But man, it wasn't easy. William Bellingham had ruled the company for decades and regime changes were never easy. I wished he was here for me to talk to, but he was off sailing around the world, enjoying his long overdue retirement with wife number five. Ruby was my actual grandmother. Younger than William by several decades, it is why I was so young as his actual granddaughter. Most people thought I was his great granddaughter or that I should be middle-aged or something.

The guy I had to fire today had all been a part of Grand-daddy's master plan for me: to go in there and set the prece-dent. I thought I did it quite well. I was probably more nervous as I entered that office than I had ever been in my life. Granddaddy had wanted me to lay low for the first week and then make a firing at my first official sighting. I knew everyone was probably calling me all sorts of horrible names right now, Angelo most especially, but Granddaddy had been right to get rid of him. Marjorie, Granddaddy's long-serving assistant and now mine, had filled me in on all the company movers and shakers and all the bad eggs. Angelo had been a bad egg and William had approved of his firing. The hiring of his replacement was left solely to me, and Marjorie had a list for that as well. I had spent the last week going over it and Alex Monaghan's name was at the top of the list. This was further enforced by his obvious dedication to his job that I had just witnessed.

Granddaddy had told me to come in early and leave late to avoid running into anyone in the first few weeks, to keep the mystery, and I had done exactly that. But while Alex had clearly been beavering away until ten thirty on a Friday night, I had been sitting in my office with my feet up reading Marie Claire for the last hour.

My heart had jumped when he stepped into the elevator with me. He was incredibly good-looking, tall with dark hair and navy-blue eyes. He rocked a suit like a god, and it made me drool just thinking about him. I knew from his personnel files that he was thirty-one, a graduate from New York University, born and bred in New Jersey. He had taken my breath away as he had smiled at me and his obvi-ous, yet sweetly shy, attraction to me was the icing on the cake. The only problem was, Granddaddy had told me no fraternizing at the office. Not only did I want to fraternize with Alex, I wanted to promote him. It was the biggest office no-no in the history of time.

My thoughts came to an end as George pulled up outside my apartment building and he opened the door for me. I smiled my thanks, with a nod to my doorman. I went to the penthouse's private elevator and flashed my key card to activate it. My apartment was another gift from my beloved grandparents. This one for my twenty-first birthday.

I'd had a dysfunctional childhood. My mother was William's youngest child and doted on, a trust fund brat who had never worked a day in her life. My dad was just as bad, living off my mother's wealth. As soon as I had been of school-going age, they had shipped me off to boarding school and then to England.

Out of sight, out of mind.

Grandma Ruby had been more of a mother to me than Suzanne, my actual mother. Ruby had done her best, but I wasn't her responsibility and when I was left at boarding school over the school vacations, I didn't blame her for forgetting to pick me up. As a result, I grew up with abandonment issues.

Big ones.

Ones I tried really hard to forget about, but they always seemed to come back to haunt me at the most inopportune moments.

I shook off the somber mood and stepped into the elevator. As I punched the button and the doors closed, I remembered Alex again. The thought of his dazzling smile gave way to the very wicked thought of him pushing me up against the mirrored walls and taking me as I wrapped my legs around him. It made my panties go damp. I crossed my legs. Oh God, I had to stop thinking about him in that way.

The doors slid open and I stepped forward. All of my needs were about to be met and I shivered at the thought of the very sexy man in my apartment.

———

"HI," I said as I kicked off my shoes and dropped my briefcase.

"Hi," he said in that deep, sexy voice.

Rex was waiting for me in the sitting room, dressed as usual in head-to-toe black to match his hair and eyes. His olive skin made me melt and I itched to get my hands on him. He stood, towering over me at six-foot-four, and moved closer. I turned on my heel and headed for the back bedroom of the penthouse. I pushed open the door to my secret lair and lit some of the candles. Rex did the same on the other side of the room. An eerie glow shone around the room, bouncing off the black-painted walls. The heavy, black, velvet drapes were pulled tight to keep out all light.

My bare feet sank into the plush, deep red carpet as I moved over to the daybed in the middle of the room. The black, wrought iron frame was scratched in places from the cuffs, and I ran my hand over the cool metal, before I stripped off my pristine white suit. Suitable for the office, but not in here. Naked was the only acceptable dress code in here and I waited as Rex removed his own clothing. I admired his rippling body as he pulled his t-shirt over his head. His ink covered most of his back and I found it as sexy as hell. My eyes lingered as he slowly turned and undid his jeans, knowing I was watching his every move. They dropped to show him commando and ready for me. My breath hitched. The angel wing tattoos on his lower abdomen were the only ones on his front and they were my favorite. I reached out to touch him but then snatched my hands back. Tonight, I was his and I wasn't allowed to touch him unless he specifically wanted me to.

I KNEW STRAIGHT AWAY that Rex didn't want me touching him. He grabbed my hands and squeezed them tightly in a warning to keep my hands to myself. He positioned me on the daybed on my knees and moved my hands onto the railing.

I had two rules in here: no talking and no kissing on the mouth. This was all about the pleasure and pain that two people could bring to each other without the need for words or signs of affection. It was all about imagination, touch and sight, or lack thereof, as Rex blindfolded me. I shivered as he cuffed my wrists to the railing. I licked my lips and wanted to take him in my mouth but until he allowed it, there was nothing I could do. He moved behind me and swept my dark hair off my shoulders, twisting it into a painful knot that he then stabbed pins into, to keep it in place. He gently touched the miniature matching angel wings on my neck, a sheer coincidence but proof of our synergy.

And then I waited. Waited for the first touch, the first stroke, or the first soft lash. I wasn't afraid. We weren't into hardcore BDSM. I had tried that, and it didn't work for me. I wanted a middle ground and my best friend (and also owner of New York's hottest sex club), Lachlan Clarke, had helped me figure out what I needed and found me a play partner with the same ideas. Rex and I had been together for eight months. We weren't *dating*. We weren't even really friends. We didn't hang out and I never spoke of him to any of my friends. Lachlan was the only one of my friends or family that knew of his existence in my life and we didn't really talk about him either. He was brooding and mysterious and I found that to be a huge turn-on. I knew very little about him in a personal sense, yet I trusted him. I'd had him investigated when we first got together, a thorough background check. I knew he worked in I.T. and was reasonably well-off, as far as the average person goes. He had no family, no criminal convictions, no debts, and hardly any digital footprint in spite of his career. We got together twice a week by prior agreement and took turns with each other. We both liked to switch and tonight I was the one bound and waiting.

REX LEFT me to stew for a while. He was completely still, just watching me. I could sense his eyes on me, and my body cried out to shift under the scrutiny, but I remained completely still, on my knees with my wrists cuffed to the bed.

After an eternity, he moved over to me and lightly brushed his hand down my back. I shivered again at his touch. His hands brushed my breasts as he fixed a pair of nipple clamps over my aching peaks. I gasped at the sensation it sent straight to my clit. His hands found my bare mound and he palmed me before sliding his fingers into me. I was so wet. He stifled a small moan as he rubbed his fingers in and over me. His fingers pressed against my lips and pushed into my mouth for me to taste myself. He pulsed his fingers in and out of my mouth. I whimpered. I needed him inside me.

He knew my thoughts and pulled away from me, causing me to wait again for the next touch. He knelt behind me on the bed and shuffled me further up. He pressed his enormous erection into my back as he bent over me and snaked his fingers down to my wet heat again. I could picture his fingers moving against me in my mind's eye and it was turning me on in all sorts of ways. I wanted a release, but every time I came close to letting go, he stopped. He was gently moving his hips in sync with his fingers, pushing his cock against me, making me feel every inch of him. My breathing grew more ragged, my pussy was soaking wet, my nipples pinched even tighter. They were close to being painful, but I reveled in the ache.

He removed his hand from me after denying me an orgasm for what felt like the millionth time. I panted with the effort of holding on. I was so ready, but to let go, before he was ready for me to, was unacceptable. Sweat sheened on my skin and as he pushed me forward and brought my hips back. My heart leapt. I grabbed the railing tighter, my palms slippery with moisture and I waited. The anticipation made it all the more intense. He pushed my face into the bed and pulled my ass higher into the air. My wrists twanged with discomfort, but I didn't care if they both broke. All I wanted was him inside me. I heard him stroking himself, the light slap, slap sounds as he made himself as hard as he could for me. I bit my lip on the inside, drawing blood but not even feeling it. Then, he finally parted me and inserted himself into my soaking wet pussy. He was rock hard, and I cried out as he rammed into me right up to the hilt.

I came suddenly with a force I didn't know was possible. He rode me through my orgasm, stoking the burning fires until I came again and again. He panted heavily and sweat on his palms as he held onto my hips. His fingers dug painfully into me as he held onto his orgasm, making this last as long as possible for me. My clamped nipples were screaming to be released. They were like two buds about to explode. Rex placed his hands on the small of my back and pushed down as he continued his onslaught. I could hear the wet sound of my honey coating him as his cock thrust repeatedly into me. My mouth watered as I thought about licking it off him and I squeezed my eyes tight behind the blindfold.

To my surprise, Alex's handsome face flashed through my mind. Oh God, now all I could think about was licking my cum off Alex's cock. That thought alone sent me over the edge a final time before Rex rammed into me and then pulled out to ejaculate all over my back. I felt the jets splat onto my skin in hot little puddles as he continued to pull on himself until he was finished.

I didn't mind if he wanted to come inside me, but this was a thing with him. He never chose to, and I was not going to pry and ask why. It was his issue and God knew I had my own quirks.

He came around quickly to uncuff me and he rubbed my wrists to get the blood flowing again. He was sweet. I could have done it myself, but he liked to look after me in these moments and I let him.

He released the nipple clamps and sucked on my aching peaks briefly before he pulled the blindfold off my eyes. He handed me a robe and I took it and pulled it on. His cum slid down my back and settled in my crack. I thought maybe he knew I liked the feel of it, sticky and cooling on my skin, and that's why he did it. Yeah, I had my own quirks, no doubt about that. I had no idea why I thought a male orgasm, and the product of that, was so erotic.

.   .   .

REX GOT DRESSED QUICKLY and then he led me out of the playroom. I closed the door quietly. He went to the elevator and turned to me with that sexy smile. He curled a piece of my wayward, sweat-plastered hair around my ear.

"I will see you on Tuesday," he said.

I nodded eagerly. I couldn't wait for my turn with him. I wanted to feel his heavy cock in my hand and taste him in my mouth. I wanted to ask him to stay so I could have a turn with him, but I stopped myself. It wasn't a part of our deal.

He leaned down to kiss my cheek. When he straightened up, he asked me, "Will you take me to the ball?"

He was referring to the ball held once a year where domineering women took their men to show off as prized pets. I had only ever heard stories. I had never attended before because I hadn't had a man to take with me. Now that I did, I was salivating at the chance to go.

"Yes," I replied, and his eyes lit up. I couldn't wait to show off my prize. I would be masked, as were all the women, but the men were not. They were also dressed only as the Mistress saw fit (which was in as little as possible, or so I'd heard) and they walked around on leashes like little dogs. I was not a Dominatrix by any stretch of the imagination, but the thought of Rex being my pet for the night pleased me far more than I thought it would.

Rex punched the button for the elevator and with an odd, lingering glance down the hallway to my actual bedroom, he stepped into it as the doors opened. I smiled at him and he gave me a half-wave as the doors closed. I followed where his gaze had gone and frowned. Did he want to go in there with me, my sanctuary where I slept, where I took my boyfriends? Rex was my only *play* partner. I was exclusive to him as he was to me with regard to that area of my life, but I did try to have my regular sex life and the two did not meet. Ever.

Well, I liked to think I had a regular sex life. After I'd met Rex, I had only managed to have one boyfriend that I'd had sex with. For some reason I just couldn't seem to hang onto a guy long enough for it to get that far. I had slept with Jason exactly once before he'd had a car accident and broke it off with me as soon he could speak. To this day, I had no idea why he had ended it.

I loved my kinky side, but I did so miss having a boyfriend to go on dates with and cuddle up to at night in bed. I was on a seriously bad streak at the moment. It had to change, and soon. I stopped to wonder what would happen to my time with Rex if I ever did find a serious boyfriend. It would no doubt have to end, and it made me wonder if perhaps I was sabotaging my own life to keep Rex in it. But then again, what if I found someone who would accept him in my life? I shook my head at both of those potentially dangerous thoughts and headed back to the playroom.

It was locked with a key card and not even the house-keeper had access to it to clean up. I did it myself. Thinking that I should probably tidy up then, I looked at the clock and saw it was nearing one in the morning. I was exhausted. I would leave it until tomorrow. I headed for a quick shower before I sank into my sumptuous, king-sized, pristinely white bed, the exact opposite to the playroom daybed. I fell into a gloriously deep, satisfied sleep.

THREE

~Alex~

I was dreaming a very hot, sexy dream about Cassandra Bellingham. She was in that clean, white business suit and I had her skirt up her hips as I slammed into her in the elevator. I was kissing her lips, inhaling that wonderful scent of hers as she wrapped her legs around me and screamed my name.

I awoke with a start. Sex dreams were not something I usually had, and my hips were moving in a pounding rhythm as if I was inside someone. My hand was pumping at my dick and I moaned.

It was only a dream, but how I wished it was a reality. I turned into the cool area of my pillow and let go of myself. Oh God, I wanted her, more than I had ever wanted a woman before. I didn't care that she was my boss. I just wanted her in my bed right then. The thought of her in bed brought the very unwelcome thought of her in bed with someone else. She, no doubt, had a boyfriend. She was too beautiful to sleep alone. I cracked my eyes open and saw that it was 8 A.M.

Shower, coffee, and back to the office.

That was my awesome day planned out.

I climbed out of bed and stretched. I always slept nude in the summer, so much freer, but obviously also easier to jerk myself off in my sleep. My cock was still hard, and it bounced as I took a step forward. I sighed. I was pathetic. Rick was right, I needed to get out more. That woman had consumed my thoughts like no other and it could only lead to trouble.

I stepped into the shower and soaped up. My still semi-hard cock twitched as I brushed it and I paused.

Oh, fuck it, I thought and grabbed it with my slippery, soapy hand. I closed my eyes. I pictured Cassandra as I stroked myself. I grew rock hard almost immediately and I groaned. I braced myself with my other hand on the wall and gripped myself. A shudder rippled through me on my first tug. I imagined that she'd caught my eye in the elevator at work and a sweet blush had darkened her cheeks. My fist pumped harder. I pictured myself crushing her against the side of the elevator and wrapping her legs around me, lifting that sexy white skirt over her hips and sinking into her. Heat swept through me, pooling in my groin. I pounded her in my mind with my eyes squeezed tight. My balls tightened and, as I imagined the sexy noises she'd make, my pleasure peaked. I stifled a groan as my orgasm swept through me, painting the shower wall in hot spurts, as I mumbled her name.

God, I wanted to see so much more of her.

I felt myself go soft and I let go, feeling a little less frustrated but a whole lot more humiliated. I doubted that she was thinking about me in the shower while she rubbed one out.

"Fuck. I need coffee," I muttered.

I finished my shower quickly and got myself ready. It was Saturday so didn't bother with a suit and tie, instead, I just pulled on a t-shirt and jeans and put my contacts in. I hated wearing my glasses, they reminded me of the geeky loser I used to be back in school. I arranged my damp, flat, dark hair into a casual, spikey look with my hair gel. I wasn't vain, well, not as vain as Rick was, but I liked to look as good as I could. Satisfied, I poured coffee in a travel mug and set about on my way. I lived in Greenwich Village, which wasn't too far from the offices in the middle of Manhattan.

LUNCHTIME CAME AND WENT, and I was close to finishing up. I leaned back in my chair and got a surprise. I looked out over the floor and saw Cassandra watching me. She started as she saw me notice her and with a quick spin, she was gone. Almost as if she had never been there. Oh God, but I wanted to follow her. I wanted to ask her why she had been watching me and for how long. It was a stupid idea, so I sighed and tried to concentrate on the remainder of my sales project.

I got it finished in under an hour and then I decided to take action. I messaged Rick: 7 P.M., Finn's, Beer.

One came straight back: You're on!

I smiled and decided that this was good. I was going to get out, get a life, and hopefully have a few laughs with my friend Maybe even meet a cute girl. It had been a while since I'd had a girlfriend, attested by my actions this morning in the shower. Cassandra Bellingham was *completely* off-limits, and I needed her out of my head.

I HEADED to the elevators and paused before pushing the button. Would she still be there? I punched it quickly and waited with bated breath. The doors opened and I peered in anxiously, but it was empty. I stepped in, disappointed, but also a little relieved, that is, until the doors closed and all I could smell was her perfume. I breathed it in and then willed the elevator to hurry up and get to the lobby. I leapt out of it as soon as I could and hurried to the doors.

Once outside, I took in the clear air, spun around and started to head home. I heard her voice - that sexy voice like honey - as I walked away and I willed myself not to look back, but I did anyway. She was talking on her phone, looking as sexy as hell in a black vest top and the tightest black jeans, with the highest heels. I felt myself stir at the sight of her again and was thankful that she didn't notice me as she slipped into the back seat of the car that pulled up. If I had just been a minute later, we would have gone down in the elevator together again. I made a noise of frustration as the car pulled away with her in it, driving her further away from me.

I chose to walk most of the way home. It took me awhile, but I didn't care. I needed to move, and I wanted to pass the time before going out later.

I went straight to the shower when I got home. I was hot and sweaty and horny. I stayed clear of my dick this time and was more determined than ever that a night out was just the ticket. Even better if I found someone I liked enough to ask out. I got dressed slowly. I was going to head out early. I needed a drink and I needed to not be alone. I chose a short-sleeved, black shirt that clung nicely to my lean, yet well-built, frame and black jeans with my biker boots. I spiked my hair again and doused myself in cologne. I grabbed my keys, wallet, and phone and left the apartment to hail a cab. I was going to drop a good few hundred dollars tonight and I might as well start now.

Instructing the driver where to go, I sat back and watched the streets roll by. Pulling up outside of my destination a few minutes later I tipped the cabbie and climbed out. The bar was already busy when I entered, and to my surprise, Rick was already there. I was over an hour early but had been prepared to sit on my own and wait.

"Hey, Al," Rick waved at me. "I wasn't even sure you would show, never mind be early." Rick slapped his hand against mine in a manly handshake and introduced me to his friends, mostly women who were eager for his attention.

Lucky bastard.

Rick was tall, blonde, well-built, and came from a well-off family. Not Bellingham wealthy, but certainly better off than my own humble beginnings. I pushed thoughts of my unpleasant childhood and family aside and ordered a beer. I sat on the stool offered by Rick and was immediately chatted up by a cute, blonde girl, who had turned her attentions away from my friend and onto me. She was pretty and had a rack that made me want to reach out and touch it. She was the perfect distraction. She was also funny and, to my surprise, smart. She was a part-time NYU student, working on the side to pay her way. We were soon engaged in a conversation about philosophy and my thoughts were nowhere near Cassandra Bellingham.

FOUR

~Cassie~

I was getting ready for my date. I had picked up the phone easily half a dozen times to cancel, but it was incredibly rude at such short notice and without a proper excuse. Besides, I needed to get Alex out of my thoughts, and Richard Pomfries IV, I had rolled my eyes excessively at that name when Grandma Ruby had mentioned it, was a good enough distraction. I chose an elegant dress in black. It dropped to my knees, with a wide halter-top that accentuated my big, but not too big, breasts and had an open back and a cinched waist. I left my hair down and I looked all right. I didn't think of myself as one of the world's great beauties, but I wasn't a troll either. I was confident enough in my looks, though, to not consider surgery as most of my friends and family already had.

I finished applying my lip gloss and picked up my purse to leave. My eyes went to the hallway leading to my playroom and I hesitated again. I could cancel and call Rex. I wondered if he would come? But did I really want him to come outside of our arrangement? Deciding to leave it, I sighed and turned back to the elevator, intent on my planned evening.

GEORGE PULLED the car up outside the restaurant and I alighted gracefully. I told him I would catch a cab home and to take the rest of the night off. As he drove off, I drew in a deep breath and looked longingly at the bar across the road. It was hopping at this hour and I wanted nothing more than to go in and chill out. I turned back to the restaurant and was ushered to my table immediately, where my date was already seated.

Richard was handsome enough, a bit like Hugh Grant with an accent to match. I found him charming and good company, enough to draw my attention away from the bar for the most part.

However, during the lulls in conversation, I noticed how tense I was. It was all about polite conversation, drinking my wine in small, ladylike sips, picking at my chicken salad with tiny, less-than-bite-size pieces. I had grown up in that elite world of extreme wealth and stiff rules on decorum and how to handle oneself, but all I wanted right then was to go across the street and guzzle back a beer, before I shoved a handful of peanuts into my mouth. I stifled a chuckle as I thought of my old Swiss Finishing School-marm's face if she saw me doing that.

Richard was quite pleasant, but less-than-exciting. I couldn't see him tying me up and giving me sweet torture, let alone me doing it to him! He was far too polite and stiff-upper-lip for that.

When he finally escorted me out of the restaurant, he offered to take me home. I declined and ignored his disappointed look, but he kissed me on both cheeks and with a little look back, he got into his car and his driver drove off. At least I could tell Grandma Ruby I had been out with him now. Hopefully, that would put to rest any more blind dates for a while. I doubted it, though. As far as the Bellingham clan was concerned, I was an old spinster already. I should already be on my second marriage, according to my cousins. I huffed as I thought of my family, and then looked across at Finn's bar. I grabbed a handful of hairpins out of my purse and I quickly worked my long hair up into a messy bun. The warm evening breeze brushed across the back of my neck and with determination in my step, I crossed the street and entered the bar. It was packed, the music was loud, the people even louder, trying to be heard over the music. I fought my way to the bar and stopped dead.

Alex.

He was there, propping up the bar and talking to a little Barbie doll-type girl. I watched as he threw his head back and laughed at something she said. My heart nearly stopped. He was magnificent. He looked like a million bucks in his tight black shirt and black jeans. Throwing caution to the wind, I stepped forward, but I was too late, the Barbie had pulled him to her and whispered seductively in his ear. His face went serious. He nodded and she took his hand and led him away.

I followed them all the way to the door that led to the bathrooms and my heart sank into the bottom of my stomach. Was he really that kind of guy? One that would pick up a woman in a bar and then go and fuck her in the bathroom? My disappointment in his actions hit me like a train. I had no idea what I was doing, but I wanted to confront him, to yell at him for being a disgusting pig or something. I stormed over to the door and wondered briefly if I had completely lost my mind. For all I knew, that girl could be his girlfriend or even his wife. I pushed open the door and saw them up against the wall in the corridor a bit further down.

I just stared at them, my jealousy overwhelming me. *I* wanted to be the one he was kissing and grinding gently against. I wanted it to be *my* hands that were pulling on his sexy ass to get him closer to me. *I* wanted to feel that hard length of him pushed up against me.

Alex pulled away as the noise from the bar echoed down the corridor and he caught my eye. He pulled away from the girl like he had been scalded. He turned his blurry gaze onto me and took a step closer, but no way was I hanging around here. I turned on my heel and hastily made my way to the exit. The crowds parted for me, as if knowing I was like a bulldozer and would just plow them down anyway if they didn't move. I yanked the door open and tumbled into the open air. I felt like such a fool, my embarrassment at my irrational jealousy heated my cheeks. I pulled my phone out and rashly called the only person I could think of who could make me feel better.

FIVE

~Alex~

I stared after Cassandra in horror. I felt awful, like I had cheated on her or something, which was totally ridiculous. She was my dream girlfriend, not my fucking real one. But her face had been a mask of disappointment in me.

Why? Why?

It was all I could think about as I got myself into motion to follow her, stumbling after her to ask her why she looked so upset with me.

I saw her moving quickly through the crowds, but I wasn't so lucky. I stumbled and lurched drunkenly and by the time I had tripped out of the bar, she was long gone. Christ, if I thought for even a second that she would be there, I would never have chatted up that girl, and I certainly wouldn't have ordered that last beer. And I *definitely* would not have taken her down to the bathroom to kiss her. She had wanted me to take her and I had gone along with it as I was pissed. I had never had sex in a public place before and even in my smashed state, I didn't think I was about to start that night. I wasn't that kind of guy. I had just wanted to get my boss out of my head for a few moments. But I couldn't do that when she was standing there staring at me macking on some other woman.

Fuck.

I was such an idiot. I couldn't go back in there; I was just going to head home like the drunken loser I was and continue to drown my sorrows there.

I heard the bar door open behind me.

"Hey," the girl said. Ella, Ellie? I couldn't even remember her name. "Was she your girlfriend?" she asked bluntly.

"Uh no, no. Just my boss," I replied, running my hand through my hair. I had nothing to lose by being honest.

"You sure about that?" she asked. "She looked pretty mad." She shoved her hands into her tight jeans, and I stared at her.

Yeah, Cassandra *had* looked mad and she had no right, I thought suddenly. I was so whipped by that woman it was pathetic. I had spoken to her once. Once! I had said less than ten words to her. This ends here.

I held out my hand to Ella, Ellie? I made a rash decision. "Wanna come back to mine?"

She hesitated but then nodded. "Yeah, just let me call my friend so she knows where I'm going." She pulled her phone out and asked for my address, which she passed it onto her friend. I was a bit insulted, but then I supposed in this day and age it was also responsible of her. She pocketed her phone and took my hand and we strolled down the street, falling into an easy conversation that soon had me laughing again.

We hailed a cab when we finally spotted a free one and soon, we were tumbling into my apartment, kissing and pawing at each other.

~Cassie~

I WAS FOCUSED. I was so mad with Alex for being there with that woman and, more importantly, at myself for over-reacting in such a strange way. I had no claim on him; he was free to do whatever he wanted and with whomever he wanted. I just wanted him to do it with me, for fuck's sake.

I stalked into my penthouse and headed straight for the playroom. Rex was waiting for me, already naked and ready for me. I shouldn't have, but I had called him, and he had come.

He watched me as I stripped off my dress and under-wear and, leaving my killer heels on, I climbed onto his lap, not even bothering with a greeting. I just thrust myself onto his huge cock, gripping his broad shoulders tightly as I rode him hard and fast. The surprise in his eyes was quickly masked by a burning desire and I felt a feeling of power rise up in me. He wanted *me*. He didn't want some Barbie bar skank that was definitely not good enough for him.

On a whim, I leaned forward and lowered my lips to his. I plunged my tongue into his mouth. He groaned softly and grabbed my hips in his strong grip. I never broke my rhythm as my tongue met his in the same intoxicating beat. I came quickly, throbbing around his shaft, coating him with my desire. Rex groaned again and released himself into me.

His eyes were closed tightly against my gaze on him, his face etched with a pain I didn't understand. But I was pleased. I had wanted him to truly let go as I had.

He then removed me from his lap, laid me down on the bed and saw to my every need and want until I couldn't even remember my own name.

I AWOKE sore and in a strange place. I blinked and realized I was on the playroom daybed. Rex had left, but he had draped a comforter over me that he had found in the sitting room, and plucked a single red rose from the hallway arrangement and left it next to me. I picked it up and inhaled its sweet scent, then I sat up and winced.

Every part of me was aching. I remembered last night with a vivid clarity. Rex had fucked me all night long. He had put me in positions I didn't know my body could get into. We had rolled around the daybed and crashed to the floor more than once. I had a bruised elbow and hip from such a fall and my head had a dull thump where the back of it had hit the metal frame. I looked down at my breasts, which were stinging slightly, and discovered they were covered in bite marks. I even had a dark purple bruise already formed from where Rex had bitten me really hard.

I had chewed on him just as savagely and wondered what *he* looked like this morning. My sex was red and raw from repeated thrusting and pounding, but in spite of the aches and pains, I had never felt so satisfied and at peace in my whole life.

I stood up and winced as my muscles complained and then I sighed. I had crossed a massive line with him last night. I hoped that we could go back to our usual arrangement, but I had my doubts. I had fucked up and if I lost him over this, I would be really upset.

I opened the door and the smell of bacon and coffee instantly hit my nose. I tilted my head and moved down the passageway to the open plan kitchen and then stopped and stared. Rex was in my kitchen, making breakfast. He turned to me as he heard me and, after a sweeping gaze over my body, lingering on my bruises, he averted his eyes and pointed to the coffee pot. I looked down at myself and realized that I was still naked. I felt oddly vulnerable and was torn between going to find a robe and gulping on a hot cup of coffee.

The coffee won out, so I slid onto a stool on the other side of the counter to Rex. At least my lower half was hidden. I didn't mind so much that my boobs were on display. What could I say? I had nice boobs.

There was a silence bordering on uncomfortable. I wasn't really surprised, as we had never been in this situation before; it was unchartered territory. I felt that I had to say something, to apologize to him for crossing the line, but I didn't know how to start.

I cleared my throat and said, "Uh, Rex?"

He turned towards me, his smoldering eyes piercing mine.

I faltered under his intense gaze and looked down.

Thankfully, he saved me from having to say anything.

"Last night we both crossed the line. It happens. We can just chalk it up to experience." He shrugged, turned his back and went back to his cooking.

"I'm sorry, Rex," I said. "It was my doing and I apologize. I shouldn't have called you last night." I traced circles on the cold, granite top, waiting for his response.

"Don't apologize," he growled at me.

My eyes shot to his back at his tone. I saw him take a deep breath and he added in a softer voice, "It was a fantastic night, but it won't happen again. We'll go back to normal on Tuesday." He said it to the frying pan, but I could sense his sorrow.

Fuck, he *did* want more from me. I had really fucked this up by offering him more, even for just one night, when I wasn't sure if I wanted to change our status.

Rex dumped the bacon, scrambled eggs and toast onto a plate and pushed it in front of me.

"You should eat," he said and then walked over to grab his leather jacket, slung over the back of the sofa. "I'll see you Tuesday." He kissed the top of my head and without another word, he left.

SIX

~Cassie~

I watched him go and felt even more awful now. I'm guessing he had hung around to make me breakfast and to reassure me that everything was okay with us. I sighed and took a sip of hot coffee. My stomach rumbled and I realized I was starving. I picked up my fork and started to shovel food into my mouth.

After my lame-ass salad last night, and my night of sexual Olympics, I was running low on fuel. Rex was really sweet. He could have just got up and left. Maybe he should have, I suddenly thought morosely.

I finished off my breakfast in record time and decided I was in need of a shower. I climbed off the stool and winced as I made my way gingerly to my bathroom. I changed my mind and decided a bath was a better idea. I had never been this sore in my life, even after my first horse riding lesson. That was brutal, but this was so much worse. After getting the water flowing into my massive Jacuzzi tub, I poured in a generous dollop of my special bath salts to help my muscles relax. Shipped over from England, it was one of my must-haves. I sank into the hot, fragrant water and relaxed.

Time to come to some decisions. Firstly, Alex was getting that promotion. I would tell him tomorrow. As soon as I had promoted him, he would be completely off-limits to me. If I started a relationship with him after I promoted him, I would never be respected, and neither would he. Both of our careers would tank, and it was so not worth it. Even for those mesmerizing, navy blue eyes. Not to mention that Granddaddy would skin me alive. Before I changed my mind, I eased myself out of the tub and grabbed my phone as I pulled my robe on. I called Marjorie and told her of my decision. Marjorie said she would arrange the meeting and the announcement. It was done now. Practically official.

Secondly, I set a reminder to myself to call Richard for a second date. I would leave it a couple of days, so I didn't look desperate or like I was too into him. It was time to forge ahead without Alex, and to keep things as they were with Rex. With my plans falling into place, I glanced at my bed and suddenly I was exhausted. I climbed into it, still in my robe, and crashed as soon as my head hit the pillow.

~Alex~

I WOKE up with a dry mouth and a nagging headache. I had a hold of myself again, stroking my erection in my sleep.

No, wait, that wasn't *my* hand. I cracked my eyes open and, staring into the bright blue eyes of the pretty blonde girl from the bar.

You stupid fucker.

I had been wasted, far more wasted than I had been in a long time. It probably didn't fall into most people's definition of wasted, but after seven beers, I was over my own personal level of tolerance.

Clearly.

I didn't *do* one-nighters. I was very much a relationship guy, so I cringed inwardly, but tried to keep a smile on my face. Christ, I couldn't even remember her name. Ella? Ellie? Elsie?

"Hey," she whispered to me, her fingers still working up and down my growing shaft.

"Hey," I croaked.

My brain scrambled to remember what had happened at the bar. I groaned again as I remembered Cassandra watching me make out with this woman and her hasty exit with me hot on her heels, only to have her disappear and blondie to follow me outside. I'd asked her back here and, well, obviously we got to know each other better. I put my hand on hers to stop what she was doing, but she was persistent and added her mouth, licking over my tip and down my length.

My dick had a mind of its own as it jerked in her mouth and hardened even more. She climbed on top of me and slid her pussy over me. She was wet enough, soft enough, hot enough, but she just wasn't the woman I wanted. Unfortunately, my dick was in control now and I shoved us over so that she was underneath me. I closed my eyes tight as I pounded into her. Cassandra's perfect face came into my mind's eye and I increased my thrusts. She cried out as she came, and I didn't last much longer. I shot my load into her and then opened my eyes quickly. Shit. What was I doing? I was having unprotected sex with a woman I didn't know. Maybe we'd had "the conversation" last night? I couldn't remember. I pulled out quickly, not that it made much difference then.

You really are a stupid fucker.

I could only hope that she was clean and protected. I remembered from the beginning of the evening that she was smart and had career plans, so surely, she was responsible with her body, right?

I felt like the biggest shit on the planet that I had used her, and I couldn't even remember her name. I had to rectify that, tactfully. I turned to her and smiled. She smiled back. She was pretty and nice from what I remembered.

"Coffee?" I asked.

"Yeah," she replied. "I'll just grab a shower if you don't mind. We could go out for coffee?"

I nodded. It sounded like a plan, a good plan, for getting Cassandra Bellingham out of my head, and to ease my guilt over screwing that girl in a drunken haze.

As she got up, I handed her my phone. "Add your number. I'd like to take you out on a real date," I said with a smile. She laughed and took it off me. I realized that I wanted to take her out to see if it led anywhere, it was the least I could do, but it was also a good way to quickly get access to her name.

Ella, I read as she handed it back to me. Yeah, I knew it was something like that.

WE HAD A VERY PLEASANT MORNING, despite my monstrous hangover. Ella had wanted to make it into a full day, but I had my presentation to do tomorrow first thing and I wanted an early night to be fresh and focused. Ella said she understood and left me to it.

I paced, showered again, paced some more, drank bucket loads of water, watched a bit of TV, then gave up and went to bed. I was completely and utterly nervous. I needed it to be better than good. Giving a presentation this close to a job opening up at the next level was going to get me watched tomorrow. I broke out in a cold sweat just thinking about it.

SEVEN

~Rex~

I sat in the dark. I didn't like the light. I downed my second Scotch of the day and it wasn't even noon yet. And I didn't usually drink. In my line of work, it was a bad idea, but I needed something, anything, to get my mind off last night. Holy hell, but I ached just thinking about it. I shook my head to clear the thoughts and poured another Scotch.

My burner cell beeped next to me and I checked the message. It was the third one I had ignored. I thought I had probably better answer it at some point.

I didn't *need* the job, but I wanted it. I worked two, sometimes three, gigs a year and it kept me in a good life. I didn't do well at nine-to-five jobs, I felt stifled and claustrophobic. I also had a problem with authority. In my line of work there was no one to answer to, there was just me and whatever target was unlucky enough to be on the other end of my

Dragunov sniper rifle. I had a cover ID to show the world, if the world came looking. I knew Cassie had looked into me. I was pleased that she had. It meant she was looking out for her safety, but she didn't have anything to worry about with me.

Being a contract killer had kind of fallen into my lap. After my dark childhood, I'd finally gotten up enough guts to up and leave my mother when I was sixteen. I got myself a fake ID and worked shitty night jobs, just to earn enough to buy my very first handgun and a membership to a gun club. I felt empowered when I had that in my hands. Never again would I be taken advantage of like my mother and her pimp had done.

I hadn't needed much food and I wasn't into drugs or booze. All I'd wanted to do was spend my money on ammo and get better at shooting. I thought, briefly, of joining the military, but it would have been too much for my lack of tolerance of other people to take. So, I practiced every day and I never missed.

I WAS APPROACHED ONE DAY, six years ago, by a shady man with the smell of money coming off him and the guy offered me a job. A job to get rid of an enemy of his. I refused, slightly horrified by the offer, but when the man told me how much he would pay, I changed my mind. Fifty grand was more money than I thought I would ever see in my life.

The man gave me half up front to plan and then the other half when the job was done. I had second thoughts at the last minute. But I kept thinking of the money and how I could leave my shitty night job.

I got it done.

I blew a hole through the guy's head and I didn't feel a thing.

The man was impressed with my ruthlessness and said he would contact me if he heard of anyone else needing a job done. Soon, I had more job requests than I knew what to do with. I refused all but the select few that called to me. The man became my contact, called himself the Captain, and I was fine with that arrangement. I didn't need to see or speak to anyone; the Captain took care of everything. My picky nature made me even more desirable and soon the Captain told me, I was the most sought-after hitman in the world.

So, a couple of jobs a year suited me. It left my days free to hit the gym and for planning an op when the need arose. And more recently, it left my days free to watch Cassandra. Ah Cassandra, I went hard just thinking about how she had come to me last night.

Funny thing was, I had been watching her on Saturday night for my job. Well, not her exactly, but her date. I had pulled up outside the restaurant in my black SUV and saw her enter. I wasn't pleased when she was ushered to the table of my intended target. Not that the job was planned for Saturday, but sitting there watching them, I had wanted to put a cap in that fucker's head more than anything else.

Cassandra was my perfection. My beautiful angel. As I watched her take dainty sips of her wine and tiny forkfuls of her salad, watched her make polite conversation and be charming and funny, I grew more in love with her than I already was. She was my princess, so perfect, so elegant out in public, but I knew her like no one else did. Her passion and sensuality, her slightly dark side that excited me like no other. Her perfect breasts and long legs. And those daisy chains. I groaned just thinking about the two tattooed daisy chains inked around each of her nipples. It was the sexiest thing I had ever seen. Her angel wing tattoo on the back of her neck came as a surprise, a smaller version of my own on my lower abdomen. When I saw it, I knew that we belonged together.

Actually, I had known we belonged together the second I saw her in Lachlan Clarke's club. I hadn't had an erection in ten years. Not one woman could get it up for me. Plenty had tried and I had tried, but after a while, I wasn't interested. I went to Lachlan's to appease a need that would likely get my ass hauled into jail if I went around beating on random women. I pushed the limits as to what I could do there and Lachlan only gave me the most depraved, broken females to play with. He knew my dark soul and accepted it, but once or twice, he had threatened to chop my hands off if I didn't pull back. I hated myself but the women adored me. I had no clue why and I didn't really care.

Sex for me was just a mess of bad, bad memories, of being pimped out by my mother when she became too worn out on crack and too old to be able to pull in the decent clients herself. She sat back and used me to make her living for her. So yeah, I wasn't interested in sex. I wasn't interested, that is, until I saw Cassandra, talking to Lachlan, wearing a black, leather bustier that barely covered her perfect tits and a skirt so tiny, I could see her ass cheeks. I felt a stirring in me and was surprised to find my leather pants had gotten tight at the front. I was getting hard. Not all the way hard, but definitely more than anything I had experienced in a long time. I knew then I had to have her. Suddenly, the need was great in me. She became my obsession. I thought of her as my redemption. I asked Lachlan to send her to me, but he refused. He said Cassandra was a princess and that I was a dog not fit to be with her. I begged and begged and asked Lachlan what I could do to make myself worthy.

"Change," he had said.

He had a soft spot for me and eventually told me he would teach me how to be with Cassandra. It took nine whole months until he said I was ready. I felt more than ready. I wanted her. I watched her, followed her everywhere. She had no idea I had become her little shadow. When she looked like she was getting serious with a guy, I would intervene, scare the guy off, and I knew she kept wondering why she couldn't hold onto someone, but she was mine.

Plain and simple.

Lachlan had eventually introduced us, and I wanted to ravage Cassandra on the spot, but she agreed to a trial run. She had specific tastes and it wasn't anything like I was used to, but Lachlan had taught me well and I knew I could please her.

On that first night, she had sunk to her knees in front of me and my fully functioning cock ached. She had sucked me into her mouth, and I had thrust once and then pulled out and came all over her chest. She was surprised, of course, but she took it all in her stride as I'd apologized profusely, feeling like an awkward teenager. She had treated me gently and when I was ready for her again, I took her and treated her just as she was, my princess.

I wanted nothing more than to be in her life permanently, so my disappointment was gut-wrenching when, at our next meeting, she had handed me a contract and a confidentiality agreement for me to sign, stating the rules. But I accepted the terms because to be without her was to be without my own life.

Eight months down the line, we were still together, and

I didn't see us ever calling it off. We were too compatible. I may have started out doing what she liked just because she liked it, but I enjoyed it and got off on it as well and all of my previously deviant behavior was long gone.

And so, my wayward thoughts came full circle back to Saturday night: watching her on her date and wanting to kill the man she was with where he sat.

I had watched his offer to take her home and I was more than relieved when she declined. I had expected her to head home. Instead, I was surprised to see her disappear across the road into the bar, only to reappear moments later shaky and upset. I was sitting several feet away from her in my SUV as her call came through and I sped off to her penthouse before I had even hung up the phone.

I loved the fact that she trusted me with a key to her place and to her playroom. I knew that none of her boyfriends had ever been given the honor. And when she had kissed me, I thought I had died and gone to heaven, but then I had come inside of her. I hadn't meant to. I didn't want to taint her with my darkness. I didn't want my evil seed inside of her.

I had crashed back into my pit of despair but then my body had taken over. She had wanted every inch of me, and I had willingly given it her, again and again and again and then I knew I had hurt her, but she didn't seem to mind. I cherished the bite marks she had given me, and I wished they could be permanent. I had watched her for the longest time as she slept and then I, too, had fallen asleep in her arms. I had slept for two solid hours, which was about an hour and a half longer than I had slept at any one time in forever. I had hung around in the morning to see if anything had changed with her, to see if she wanted a proper relationship with me now, but as she stood there looking awkward and vulnerable, I knew that nothing had changed.

Over my breaking heart, I had spoken first and told her it was no big deal and she accepted it, and I hated that.

I poured another Scotch and I answered the message. Yeah, I was taking the job even though I had already had two this year and it was only July. I was taking out that motherfucker before he got any closer to my beautiful angel. Hell, I would even do it for free. I operated on a "don't ask, don't tell" basis, but I wanted to shake the hand of whoever wanted him taken out. The Captain replied straight away and then I switched the burner off. I kept my real phone on all the time just in case Cassandra called me. I would drop everything if she called, not that she would. She had only ever called me once outside of our arrangement and that was last night.

EIGHT

~Alex~

I tossed and turned all of Sunday night and was up with the birds to get ready for work. I was in as the cleaning staff were finishing up and I went to the conference room to make sure everything was in order. Then, I sat at my desk and waited, just waited until 9 A.M. and it was time.

I entered the conference room with my head down and I smelled her perfume before I saw her. That intoxicating scent that made me weak at the knees. I looked up and swallowed loudly. Cassandra was sat at the head of the table, watching me through narrowed eyes. She was dressed today in a black suit and her raven hair was piled up high on her head in a tight bun. She looked spectacular and totally out of my league. She sat stiffly and her expression didn't change as my eyes met hers.

Gary, the senior V.P. for my section, jumped up from

his seat next to her and made the introductions. I just nodded, speechless, and smiled briefly before I turned away from her steely gaze.

Christ, she looks like she hates me, I thought as my palms started to sweat. Fuck, I so did not need her in here today. This presentation had to be perfect. My career depended on it. Maybe that's why she was there, to see if I was V.P. material. That thought eased me. It was exactly what I needed to turn around again with my charming smile and my easygoing nature that got clients lining up for me.

I looked at everyone in the room and then started to speak, giving them each my undivided attention for a few moments. Everyone except her that is. I knew that if I looked at her, I would trip over my words, forget my carefully prepared presentation, and make a total ass out of myself. I could sense that she never took her eyes off me and it unnerved me, but I pushed it away. After the hour was up and I was shaking hands with the potential client, I chanced a quick glance at her. The praise of the client fell on deaf ears as I just stared at her, as she did to me. She broke away first and I drew my attention back to the client.

I saw her wince as she rose stiffly, and I wondered if she was okay. I was going to ask her, needing to speak to her, but as I took a step forward, Marjorie stepped up to me.

She handed me an envelope, as the client left. "Read it when you get back to your office," she whispered. "And keep it to yourself."

I clutched it in my hand and nodded at her. I knew it was from Cassandra, I could smell her perfume all over it. I had to find out what that scent was. I hurried back to my office and closed the door. I ripped the envelope open, not knowing what to expect, but hoping it was an invitation to a secret rendezvous. I was wildly disappointed when it was a typed letter on official letterhead requesting my presence in her office at 11 A.M. She had signed it herself with a flourish, her letters all round and curvy. I ran my finger over it and then stuffed it back in the envelope. I popped it into my inner jacket pocket so that I could smell her all the time. I knew I was a sap, but she just had that effect on me.

I SAT and watched the clock. It felt like a million years until it reached ten minutes before eleven. I got up, walked over to the elevators, and punched the button to go up. I had never been to the top floor before. Never had a reason to. I climbed in and only then began thinking what a lazy ass I was since I could have taken the stairs, I went up one floor. The doors dinged open and I stepped out onto a very plush floor. Nothing like the one downstairs; this was expensive, elegant, executive.

Just like her.

I hovered for a moment not knowing what to do, when Marjorie bustled towards me.

"Follow me," she murmured.

She ushered me into Cassandra's office and closed the door.

I gulped.

She was sitting behind her large desk looking like a schoolmistress and I felt very much like the naughty schoolboy.

"Sit," she said.

I did as I was told.

She smiled then and I relaxed and took in her beauty.

"Relax, it's good news," she said.

I nodded. I knew then that the promotion was mine. "Okay," I said. I had fuck all to add to that like the dumbass that I was.

She must have read it on my face. "Mr. Monaghan, I am pleased to offer you the position of junior Vice-President," she said, her voice like honey, her green eyes fixed on mine with an intensity that unnerved me.

I cleared my throat. "Thank you, Miss Bellingham," I said, with what I hoped was a dazzling smile. "I am honored that you thought of me for this position, and I accept."

I wanted to add how it was everything that I had worked towards for the last few years, but her face was a mixture of disappointment and relief that I had accepted, which made me wonder as to the cause of that. It killed off any other words that might have come out of my mouth when she stood up, came to stand in front of me and held out her hand for me to shake.

I stood as well and as soon as my, hand touched hers something idiotic came over me and I pulled her to me and gave her a kiss on her lips. She fell into it for a moment before she slapped her hand up to my chest and pushed me back.

"Mr. Monaghan, what are you doing?" she asked me as she stepped back, slightly flushed.

I cringed; I had no idea what the fuck I was doing. "I-I'm sorry," I stammered my apology and she stepped back even further, bumping into her desk. Her cheeks were flushed, and I was sure that mine were flaming.

She turned and picked up a folder from her desk and shoved it at me. "These are all the details. Anything you need to know, ask Gary," she said quickly before she walked back to her chair and sat down, burying her head in her laptop.

"Thanks," I muttered and beat a hasty retreat, the folder held up against my face as I almost ran past Marjorie to the stairs this time. I took them two at a time and then kept on going. I wasn't ready to go back to my desk yet. I desperately needed a workout to run off my tension, and thought briefly of going to the gym, but it was the middle of the workday and I had just been promoted. Not exactly a slick move. And speaking of stupid moves, what had I been thinking, doing that to her? I was mortified. I didn't think I would ever be able to face her again.

I had run down seven flights of stairs and had calmed a little bit, so I slowly climbed back up them to go to my desk. The news had already filtered down and the next hour was spent with congratulations and colleagues coming to check out my office, just in case they got promoted into my old job. I practically got kicked into my new corner office after a heated argument about who was going to get *my* job.

THE DAY DRAGGED on and finally it was time to leave. I made sure that most of the floor had gone home before I left and then I headed to the gym. It was located not far from the offices. I hadn't been in a while, but I had a gym bag on hand in my office.

I changed and headed to the running machines.

"Damn," I muttered. That guy was here. He seemed to live here. Every time I came, that guy was here. He freaked me out. He was so intense it was like you could feel it radiating off him and his stare was completely blank. He never spoke to anyone and no one ever spoke to him. I took the machine the furthest from him and got to running.

An hour later when I got off. I was thankful that the guy was nowhere to be seen and I headed home, feeling good and not quite so stupid about that kiss. Running off my frustrations had worked a treat and I was determined to just forget it and go back to the office tomorrow as if nothing had happened.

NINE

~Cassie~

I couldn't stop thinking about Alex's lips on mine. They were so soft and yet the kiss had been firm. I had wanted more, so much more, but somewhere I had found the willpower to push him away and I regretted it. I sighed as I packed up my briefcase. A few more days of this staying-late business and then I could start on some regular hours. I decided there and then to call Richard and arrange another date. I had wanted to wait another day or so, but after that kiss, I needed it to be now. I picked up my phone and he answered on the third ring. His accent made my stomach flutter and I thought that was good. I couldn't see him tomorrow as it was Tuesday, but I made a date with him for Wednesday. Feeling slightly better about the Alex situation, I made my way downstairs and home.

THERE WAS a hand-delivered envelope waiting for me when I arrived at the penthouse and I recognized the sharp handwriting instantly. It was from Lachlan. I tore it open and, as expected, it was the invitation to the Mistresses' Ball in a few weeks. I grinned as I thought of going to that with Rex. He was a hot, ripped, brooding, sexy beast and I couldn't wait to show him off. It would be our first public appearance together, but I would be behind a mask so no one would know it was me. It was perfect.

I looked at the date again and then frowned. It looked familiar. I grabbed my diary and flicked through it and then slumped.

"Crap," I said, thoroughly annoyed. It was the same date as the Bellingham Corporation Annual Ball. I had to go, I had no choice, especially seeing as the company was mine. My disappointment weighed heavily on me as I started to realize that my life wasn't my own anymore. I had been handed the mantle and I had to accept it. I would decline with Lachlan tomorrow and tell Rex that I couldn't go. I flopped into bed, angry and disappointed and more than a little frustrated.

TEN

~Alex~

I had managed to avoid Cassandra all day. Not surprising, really, as I was still on the floor below hers and had no need to interact with her. My plan of action was to just pretend like the kiss had never happened the next time I saw her and hopefully she would as well. She had made her feelings perfectly clear, so I had to move on from this ridiculous obsession.

I HIT the gym again after work and it was slammed. I cringed when I saw the only free treadmill was next to "that guy." Oh, how I really didn't want to go and run next to him. Not only because of his menacing air, but because I would also look completely lame next to him. The dude was a god. We weren't supposed to go shirtless in this gym, but I didn't think anyone was going to argue the point with *him*. The guy was ripped, not surprising really, seeing as he seemed to live in here. I was toned, I had a nice six-pack that I was proud of, but any man would feel inferior standing next to that.

Well, it was either get on or get out, so I swallowed my discomfort and climbed aboard. The guy glanced briefly at me and I shivered before I yelled at myself for being a wuss.

I started to clock up the miles when my gaze drifted over to my right in the mirror. I was casting glances at the god-guy I couldn't help myself, when I caught sight of something that nearly made me go flying backwards.

Was that a bite mark?

No, there were *several* bite marks, bruising and going yellow, but definitely bite marks. And scratches too. All the way down his chest.

Christ, dude was into some kinky shit. I was a bit of a prude; I knew that. Up until the other day, I had only ever been with four women, women that I had been in relationships with. And then the disastrous mistake with Ella made five. I liked sex, of course I did, but all that biting and scratching and tying people up was not up my alley. But it didn't surprise me that this guy was into all that.

I knew I was staring, and judging, when the guy turned to me and said, "Something I can help you with?"

Surprised, I lost my pace on the treadmill and had to scramble to stop myself from falling over.

"Uh," I muttered like a fool and then carried on speaking anyway, "Quite some hellcat you've got." I pointed to the guy's chest and he looked down. His hard gaze softened slightly as he muttered something that sounded like, "She's an angel," before he turned his eyes back to the mirror, ignoring me again.

Oh yeah, I thought. I knew the type: princess by day, slut by night. Trust fund girls who played up to their daddy's ideal on the outside but rode the bad boy on the sly. I'd bet my entire month's salary that this guy had them crawling all over him. Literally, going by his marked skin.

"I'm Alex, by the way," I said to the guy, although I had no idea why I kept blurting my name out to people this week, like I was that loser kid trying to make friends at school again.

After a moment, where I thought he either hadn't heard me or was ignoring me, the guy growled back, "Rex."

I bobbed my head. At least I had a name for him now.

"See ya," Rex added as he leapt off the running machine and headed to the changing rooms. A man of few words.

I should have known I wouldn't get much out of him. I caught a few of the other guys staring at me, impressed that I had spoken to that scary-ass motherfucker that everyone avoided. I gave them a smug grin, feeling brave, and also, quite ridiculous, and went back to my workout.

~Rex~

I DISAPPEARED QUICKLY. I had no idea why I was talking to that Alex guy. I never spoke to anyone and certainly didn't offer up my fucking name. Maybe it was because I was nervous. It was Tuesday and I was due at Cassandra's in a few hours. I had half a mind to cancel. I had even thought that *she* would cancel. I kept checking my phone, but nothing had come through yet. In fact, I decided finally, if she did cancel, I would ignore it and turn up anyway. It was her night with me so the ball would be in her court, and that made me feel better. If it had been the other way around, I probably would have bailed.

I couldn't wait to see her, though, and I thought about her the whole way home. I showered and changed and was about to head back out when I saw an envelope had been slipped under my door. I knew what it was straight away: the invite to the ball. I ripped it open and was excited that Cassandra had agreed to take me. I went and placed it carefully on my desk and my eyes caught the folder that had been delivered yesterday. In it, was everything I needed to know about my current target. I hoped that Cassandra stayed away from the guy. I didn't really want her being anywhere near that job. I grabbed my keys and her key card and headed for the penthouse.

I never violated her privacy at home. I could have come and go as I pleased since she gave me access a couple of months ago, and it had occurred to me on more than one occasion to rig her place up so I could watch her 24/7. But I'd always stopped myself from doing it. Although, I had on one occasion arrived quite early and gone through her bedroom. I'd been fascinated at how immaculate it was. So completely different to how I knew her. I knew that if I ever got her in there, it would be a completely different experience. I was unsure whether or not that pleased me. I didn't like to think that I didn't really know her and only saw one side of her. I had also wondered, more than once, since Sunday morning that if I had waited for her in the sitting room instead of in the playroom, would she have taken me to her bedroom instead?

I pulled into her parking garage in my black Mustang. I didn't like to bring the SUV here in case she recognized it somehow as the one that followed her all over town. Not that she knew she was being followed, I didn't think. I would have imagined she would have set up some kind of security had that been the case, but she went about her business as she always did.

A pang of nerves hit my stomach as I climbed out and headed for the elevator. It took its time coming, which meant that it had come from the top floor.

She was home already.

ELEVEN

~Cassie~

I had been a nervous wreck all day. I had typed up about three different messages to Rex canceling tonight, but I knew he would know it was because of Saturday no matter what excuse I put, so I deleted them all unsent. I hated that it was my turn. If it had been *his* turn, I would have been able to relax. I had no idea what to do with him. Just go back to normal like nothing had ever changed between us? It was probably for the best. I also decided to wait until *after* to tell him I couldn't go to the ball. He would be disappointed, and I didn't want to ruin the mood even further. That was if he even showed up. I had half hoped he would call and cancel.

It was getting late and I had no idea what to wear for him. I opened my closet and pushed all the clothes out to the sides and stepped in. I slid back the fake wall and stepped further into the closet. This was where all of my kinky stuff was kept. The last thing I needed was my housekeeper or Grandma Ruby to see the array that was currently in front of me. My eyes quickly scanned over all the outfits that I had and then decided as they landed on the perfect top.

It was a black, leather bra top with two cut-out holes for my nipples to poke through. I knew Rex loved my daisy chains and these would be on show. Actually, I hadn't come across any man that had seen my daisy chains and didn't love them. It drove them crazy. It was one of the reasons I had chosen to have them done. Lachlan had gone with me a few years ago and it had hurt like hell but had so been worth it. My angel wings were older. I'd had them done at a place in London that didn't bother checking for an ID when I was fifteen. Only Lachlan knew the reason I'd had them done and I doubted I would tell anyone else. It wasn't anyone's business.

Now that I had my top in place, I picked a skirt. A tiny, tight, black skirt that showed off my ass and did not leave anything to the imagination. I added a pair of what I liked to think of as "porn shoes". Those crazy high heels with a massive platform in patent black, open toe and with a buckle. I had no intention of removing my shoes that night, so they were perfect. As I turned to exit the secret closet, on impulse, I grabbed a riding crop, and then closed up and went to wait for him.

I lit the candles and then sat on the daybed to wait. I crossed my legs and leaned back, but then corrected my position. It looked too forced, too posed.

My heart leapt into my throat as I heard the elevator doors ding open and then his heavy footfalls on the hardwood floor. He paused and then I heard him come towards me. He pushed the door open further and his eyes smoldered at my very sexy outfit, lingering on the riding crop with a slightly raised eyebrow. He knew he was in for it and I felt a power rush go through me.

He had discarded his leather jacket and was dressed, as usual, in head-to-toe black, with his biker boots in place. How he wasn't sweating to death, I didn't know. He crossed the threshold and went over to the corner to undress.

I watched him. God, how I loved to watch him undress. It was like watching a Christmas present being unwrapped every single time. Even though I knew what was under the wrapper, he still took my breath away when I saw him. I hastily stood up and went to the drawer to get the cuffs that had long enough chains that I could attach him to either side of the daybed. He sat without my instruction and watched me closely as I snapped the left cuff into place on the bed and then onto his wrist, followed by the right one. I leaned over and took his heavy cock in my hand and brought him to attention. It didn't take long, and then I walked around the back of him to make him wait.

I studied his back as I waited. It was covered in tattoos of all designs, but the one that interested me the most, because it was so unusual and clearly unfinished, was on his left shoulder. It was a circle about six centimeters across with tiny little lines, almost like a clock's markings but a lot closer together, etched around the inside. I leaned closer and gently touched the first line. He growled in protest and pulled his shoulder away from me.

I growled back at him and roughly pulled him back.

I touched each one in turn and counted fourteen in total. His back was stiff under my touch and I noticed that his erection had disappeared as I had counted off the lines. What on Earth did they mean that they could have such an effect on him? I really should learn more about him, I resolved.

I snatched up the riding crop and walked around to face him. His gaze was lowered, he didn't want to meet my eyes, so I chucked him under the chin with the tip of the crop. His blazing eyes met mine and I almost flinched at what I saw in them. Darkness like I hadn't seen before and I had seen my fair share. It worried me slightly, until he altered his expression and my lust welled up at his look of desire. I ran the crop down his shaft and over the tip. It hardened and grew in response. I smiled wickedly. I raised my arm and brought the crop down with a swift lash to his chest. He winced in surprise and tensed up. His jaw was tight and his face grim, but he didn't lose his erection, so he wanted it. I did it again and again and I heard him stifle a moan, but I knew it wasn't of pain, it was of desire.

It spurred me on. I leaned forward and broke my own rule by whispering in his ear, "Do you want it harder?"

Rex's black eyes burned through mine. He nodded and braced himself. I felt another rush of power slice through me. I raised the crop and brought it down on his chest as hard as I could. That one left a red welt and I stopped in shock. I didn't want to hurt him like that. I knew he could take a lot, he was a big, strong guy, but as the dark purple bruise started to form, I hesitated. He sensed me falter and grabbed tighter onto the chains, again bracing himself, his actions telling me it was okay, and he wanted me to do it.

I'd started this out as a bit of fun, but now it had turned into something darker. Something I wasn't sure I wanted to continue. The only problem was, I had no idea what to do next. I stopped thinking and tossed the crop aside. I knelt in front of him and pushed his legs apart. I pressed my lips to where I had bruised him, and I heard his sharp intake of breath. His heart started hammering under my lips. I dragged my tongue down to his nipple and licked it, before I sucked on it. His cock bounced slightly against my stomach and I was secure again. My confidence returned, so I pushed him back to the bed and took him in my mouth. He was rock hard and salty on my lips. I devoured him. I wanted him to come in my mouth so that I could taste him, but before he did, he sat up suddenly, pushing me back enough for me to lose my grip on him. He grunted as he came then, splashing on my chest and his thighs.

I was disappointed; I'd thought after Saturday that maybe he was over whatever his issue with this was. Obviously not, though. But screw that, I thought, as I let him finish and then bent over and licked up every last drop from him and then took my finger and wiped myself clean. His look of anguish and desperation intrigued me, but when I licked my lips like I had just tasted nectar from the gods, his eyes went straight to my mouth and he started to lengthen again. I wasted no time climbing onto his lap. I gripped his shoulders tightly and sank down onto his cock. I pleased myself twice with it, before I climbed off. I felt awful about not letting him finish that time, but that was his punishment for denying me his taste and as I looked at him, I knew he knew it.

I uncuffed him and stood back to see if he would take care of himself. When he didn't and he stood, I stepped back further and felt even worse. I had used him and that just felt wrong. The fact that Rex had *let* me use him didn't go any way to making me feel any better. I just stood and watched him as he got dressed and then he turned and walked away. As soon as he was across the threshold, I grabbed his hand.

"Rex."

He looked at me and said, "Don't feel bad, Angel. I deserved it, and far worse."

"What?" I asked, confused. What was he talking about?

"I'll see you on Friday," he said instead and then I remembered that I had bad news.

"Rex, wait. About the ball. I can't go," I blurted out before he left.

He hesitated, his hand hovering over the elevator button. "Oh," he said flatly and punched it harder than was necessary.

"Rex," I said again as the doors slid open. "Wait, let me explain."

"No need," he said shortly, as he stepped inside.

I slapped my hand up to stop the doors from closing and I said, "Listen to me. I have another function on that night. One that I cannot get out of. I'm sorry."

He glared at me for a moment before he asked, "What time does your other function start?"

"Seven thirty," I replied.

"The ball doesn't start until ten," he said.

"I know, but I can't just leave in the middle of my other event. It's work," I said.

"Why not?" he asked.

I just looked at him as a thought crossed my mind. "Very well," I said as haughtily as I could while standing there with my nipples and ass on show. "I will leave at ten thirty and we will just have to be late."

"See? That wasn't so difficult now was it?" he asked with a slightly raised brow at my tone. He smiled a very sexy smile at me as the doors closed, removing him from sight. I huffed out a breath. How was I going to explain my getaway to the board of directors? Feign illness?

I TIDIED UP THE PLAYROOM, closed the door quietly and made my way to my bedroom. My phone rang and I frowned at it. It was past midnight. Who would be calling me at this time? The number was blocked and that caused me more consternation. I ignored it but it continued to ring. I switched it off and then nearly jumped out of my skin when the landline went off. No one *ever* rang that number. I didn't even know anyone who had it. The answering machine picked up, the default setting that just asked the caller to leave a message, and a distorted voice said, "Cassandra, Cassandra. I know you are home and what you are doing. You are playing a dangerous game. You will get burned." They hung up and I gulped. What was all that about? I felt a frisson of fear slide down my back. I ripped the phone out of the wall and went to make sure the front door was locked. No one except the housekeeper used the door, which led out to the main elevator, so it was securely fastened. I still slid the bolt into place, hoping that I would remember to undo it in the morning, or the housekeeper wouldn't be able to get in.

I walked quickly to my room, closed the door and locked that too. I really should have a shower, but I was too scared after the ominous phone call. The last place I wanted to be, if someone broke into my home, was in the shower. In the end, I told myself I was being ridiculous and stepped under the jets. Exactly ten seconds later, after the quickest wash in history, I leapt back out and turned it off, feeling like a fool. But a scared fool. That phone call had really unnerved me. I crawled into bed and pulled the duvet up around my ears in a useless defense, and then I just lay there until exhaustion pulled me under.

TWELVE

~Rex~

I climbed into my Mustang and drove out of the parking garage. I felt very frustrated, but I wasn't going to do anything about it. If Cassandra had wanted me relieved, she would have let me be. I wasn't going against her wishes, so it would just have to wait until Friday. The street was deserted as I pulled out onto it, except for someone standing in the shadows. An ordinary person probably wouldn't even have noticed them, but I had an eagle eye and was as paranoid as they came. I drove slowly past the person, dressed in baggy jeans and a jacket with the hood pulled low over their face. They stepped back further into the dark and disappeared, but not before I saw them looking up at the apartment building.

Cassandra's apartment building. I circled around the block and parked. I grabbed my Glock from under the seat and stepped out of the car. I had a creepy feeling that whoever that was, had bad intentions towards Cassandra. I didn't know how I knew that; I just did. I did a quick sweep, but the person was long gone. I climbed back into the car and then just sat there. I wasn't leaving her unprotected. I was used to sitting and waiting for long periods, so I had no problem with just staring at the apartment building's entrance until the sun rose. Her driver would be along shortly to wait for her, and I knew that he would make sure she was escorted safely to work. That was what I paid the man for, after all. George also knew that if anything happened to her on his watch, I would kill him without a second thought. That was probably more of an incentive than the cash. I waited until I saw George pull up and get out of the car to wait for her and I drove off. One thing was very clear to me, and regardless of my feelings over violating her privacy, I was installing cameras in her apartment that day. That way I could watch her and know that she was safe and if she was in danger, I could be there to help her.

I drove the short distance to my apartment, got what I needed for surveillance and went back to wait until she had left for work. She drove off and I pulled into the parking garage. I went up to her penthouse and set about to work. I installed tiny cameras in every room and from every angle except the playroom, as she only went in there with me, and the bathroom. No one deserved to be spied on while they were in there, and besides, I would see an intruder long before they reached her in there anyway. I lingered in her bedroom and wondered again what it would be like to have her in here, what she would be like in here. I reached out to touch the crisp white duvet but quickly drew my hand back. My evil coated my skin like a black oil, and I didn't want to taint her beautiful, white bed with my darkness. I heard a key going into the lock at the front door and I quickly headed back to the elevator. There were three locks to undo so I got the doors closed just in time before the housekeeper walked in.

THIRTEEN

~Alex~

I was staring at Ella across the table. She was talking about
something, but I had no idea what. I hadn't heard a word of
what she said since we sat down. I was trying, I really was,
but I just wasn't that into it.

She stopped speaking and was staring back at me expec-
tantly. Had she just asked me a question? I blinked and
smiled apologetically.

"I'm sorry," I said. "I just have a lot on my mind at the
moment."

I didn't. All I had was *one* thing on my mind and it
wasn't the woman sat across from me. It was the woman
who was seated about four tables over, in a beautiful, green
dress that matched her eyes, having dinner and polite
conversation with some guy who looked like Hugh Grant. If
Cassandra had spotted me, she hadn't reacted, so I, too, had
ignored her. These last weeks had been torture for me. Ever

since that stupid kiss in her office, I had been a wreck. I took most of my frustration out at the gym and the rest I took out by screwing Ella. I disliked myself immensely for using her this way, as I wasn't that guy. I kept telling myself that, but I knew then that I was. I was using Ella to forget Cassandra and that was just wrong. I promised myself every day that I would break it off with her, but then what? So, I could sit at home alone or, worse, at the office?

"We can leave if you want?" Ella said eventually, with a small, tight smile.

"Yeah, let's," I said and called for the check. She looked disappointed until I added, "We'll go back to my place for dessert."

Her eyes lit up and I felt a pang in my stomach; I was a douche.

We made a quick exit and soon I had her under me in my bed, using her for my own pleasure with another woman on my mind. I rolled off her when I'd finished and sighed. She snuggled into me and I let her only because I felt bad. God, I was pathetic. I needed to get a life. I made a decision, one I probably should have thought about a bit more, but then the question was out, and I couldn't take it back.

"Do you want to go to this work party thing with me the week after next?" I cringed inwardly because making plans with her for a couple of weeks away was a dumb move.

"Sure," she said. "What is it exactly?"

I told her about the annual Bellingham Ball and her eyebrows went up. "A ball? That sounds fancy."

I shrugged. I had never been before, I was only invited this year because of my recent promotion. "It is black tie," I said. "It's okay if you don't want to go." I gave her an out and hoped that she took it.

"No, it sounds like fun," she replied.

I sighed again and reached over to show her the invite.

"I'll have to go shopping. I don't have anything to wear," she said.

I smiled at her and pulled her to me again. I feigned sleep until she eventually dropped off. I got up and did my nightly ritual in the shower, thinking of Cassandra as I jerked off, coming with a groan, my eyes tightly closed so I could see her face. God, I wanted to see so much more of her. I could tell she had a body to die for under those perfectly cut suits and elegant dresses. I had seen the evidence tonight in that green dress.

I dried off and climbed back in bed with Ella. I closed my eyes and willed for sleep to come.

I AWOKE with a start when my alarm went off. I forgot I had set it super early as I had planned on hitting the gym before work.

Ella stirred next to me and cracked her eyes open. "Ugh, what time is it?" she asked.

"Early," I said. "I was going to go to the gym before work."

She smiled seductively. "If you stay here, I can give you a workout."

I smiled back at her. I must be the stupidest man on the planet that I would rather go running on a treadmill than stay in bed with her. She was pretty, she had a killer body, and she was sweet and fun. "I'm meeting a friend there," I lied. "Next time."

She looked disappointed, so I kissed her and said, "Don't forget to go shopping for a dress."

The distraction worked like a charm and she grinned excitedly.

I quickly got dressed and kissed her again before I left.

"I'll call you later," I said. I wasn't too bothered about leaving her in my apartment. Even if she did go rooting through my things, all the private stuff was locked away and the rest was just boring house stuff.

I RAN ON THE TREADMILL, lost in my thoughts. I was surprised when Rex got onto the one directly next to me in this deserted gym. Actually, I was more surprised that he hadn't been there when I'd arrived.

"Hey," I said.

"Hey," Rex said, keeping his eyes in front.

I watched as he took his shirt off and punched in the time on the running machine. I blinked rapidly as I saw what was marking his chest that time. A big, black bruise right across his chest where it looked like someone had whipped him. Christ. What was this guy into? I also noticed the faint bruises on his wrists, and I started to sweat as my imagination went into overdrive. I saw Rex chained to a wall, while some woman in black leather whipped his ass.

I gulped and quickly turned away, pushing away the very real memory of my past. It was none of my business what the guy did with his sex life. If that was even what that was. He probably had a perfectly innocent reason, but I couldn't stop my runaway mouth as I blurted out, "The angel again?" as I pointed to Rex's chest. I mean, seriously. If the guy didn't want people to see it, he shouldn't have taken his fucking shirt off in public.

Rex looked down and then at me. His pace never faltered. "Yeah, what's it to you?"

I gulped. Well, I started this so I might as well finish it. "Just curious." I shrugged casually, but I so did not want to meet that woman. She sounded like she was pretty wild.

Rex grunted at me and then ignored me for the rest of the hour.

I was startled when, as I finished, Rex did as well and regarded me with a close look. "You don't speak about this again," Rex said in a perfectly normal tone, but the look in his eyes sent a shiver down my spine. "What my woman does to me is none of your business."

"Got it," I said with a nod.

Rex nodded back and then left me staring after him, wondering what kind of woman would hook up with a guy like him anyway. She must have a serious grudge against her daddy or a couple of screws loose. Or possibly both.

I GOT into work a few minutes early and opened my email. The first one that jumped out at me was a meeting scheduled for later that day with the executives.

"Ah, hell," I muttered.

I was going to have to sit across from Cassandra at that meeting. I had dreaded this, but better to get it over with, I supposed.

The day crept by slowly and when the time for the meeting came, I reluctantly went to the conference room. She was there already, and I ignored her. I could feel her eyes on me but kept mine firmly averted. She eventually turned away from me. I wanted nothing more than to turn to her and talk to her, but I daren't. I would probably end up kissing her again like the lovesick asshole that I was.

THE MEETING ENDED AN HOUR LATER, and I beat it back to my office. I called Ella and decided to make a go of this, properly. I couldn't go around mooning over Cassandra Bellingham for a single day longer.

THE SATURDAY of the ball came around fairly quickly since I had decided to focus on Ella a bit more. We had spent almost every night together and I was starting to really like her. We had a good time and she made me laugh. I had stopped my nightly shower ritual exactly five days ago. I felt no need to do it and I finally felt like I was moving on from my ridiculous crush.

Ella came out of the bedroom and twirled in a circle for me.

"Wow," I said. "You look great." I meant it. She looked really sexy in the slinky black dress. I ignored the tag that I could see sticking out of the back, but gently shoved it down as I ushered to the door.

"Thank you," she said and blushed.

She had gotten ready at my place as she was coming back later anyway. She lived a bit further out of the city and it just made more sense.

I held my arm out for her to take. Ella accepted it with a smile, and we made our way down to the waiting car that had been sent for us. She was really impressed as she slid into the back seat and I could tell that she was excited. I wasn't too bothered about this, but as it was my first one, I had to show my face.

We waited our turn in the line of cars to get out at the Four Seasons and I helped her out. She was in awe, but I just wanted to head to the nearest bar.

After knocking back a couple drinks, my eyes inadvertently scanning the crowd. I relaxed and started to enjoy the evening. I wasn't watching the clock as I thought I would be, but maybe that was due to the alcohol.

As I waited my turn at the bar again, having left Ella hovering somewhere near some tables, I smelled Cassandra's perfume before I saw her.

I turned slightly to my left and there she was. My mouth dropped open as I took her in. She looked like a frickin' princess. Her pale pink dress was strapless and tight to her waist, but then puffed out into a pale pink cloud of material embedded with crystals that twinkled as she moved.

"Hello, Alex," Cassie said to me as she smiled at my reaction to her.

I opened and closed my mouth while I tried to speak, but it took me a few tries.

"Hi," I eventually got out. "Wow, you look incredible," I added without thinking.

"Thank you," she said, inclining her head gracefully.

The waft of her perfume filtered over me and I had to ask, "That perfume you wear, what is it?"

She looked startled by the random question, but then said, "Chanel No. 5. It's an unusual choice for my age, but I like it."

"So do I," I said and breathed in like a fool. I knew there and then that I was so not over my crush and there was no point in denying it anymore. "Dance with me." I held my hand out for her, forgetting all about my drink.

Cassie hesitated and looked at my outstretched hand. Oh, I wanted her to take it so I could whisk her around the dance floor.

I was about to pull my hand back, after what seemed like an awkward forever, but then she grabbed it and looked into my eyes.

"Yes," she said quietly. "I would like that."

My knees went weak as she turned and led *me* to the dance floor. Her hair was coiled up high on her head and I could see a little pair of angel wing tattoos on the back of her neck. I almost drooled. I wasn't that into tattoos on women, but that was the sexiest thing I had ever seen. I reached out to touch it, unable to stop myself. She whirled around as my fingers touched her neck. I snatched my hand back with an apologetic look.

"Sorry," I mumbled, hoping that she wouldn't think I was a crazy man and still dance with me. "They're beautiful," I added and could kick myself. My confidence around that woman was non-existent.

Cassie smiled at me. I know I looked like an awkward teenager, and thought it was perhaps a pity smile. However, she tightened her grip on my fingers and said, "It's okay. I just wasn't expecting it. Do you really think so?"

FOURTEEN

~Cassie~

I leaned in closer to him as I said it. I didn't know what I was doing. I was supposed to be staying away from him and here I was throwing my most seductive look at him. Not that he noticed because his eyes were fixed firmly on my cleavage. I didn't mind that. I kept thinking what that perfect mouth of his would feel like on my skin. I also couldn't help wondering what he would make of my daisy chains.

Oh, Cassie. Stop that.

"Yeah," he croaked out, as I was waiting for his answer. "It's sexy."

"Mm," I said slowly. "If you like that, you will love..." I trailed off and looked down. His eyes followed where I was looking, and I could see a thousand possibilities fly through his head.

"Show me," he whispered boldly.

I laughed and shook my head. "Ah no, Mr. Monaghan. You don't get to see those ones. I will leave it to your imagination," I teased.

"That's a dangerous game, Ms. Bellingham," he said, his confidence seemed to have returned now that I was flirting with him as well.

"Those are the best kind," I said as I lowered my eyes. Oh, I really had to stop this flirting.

Alex pulled me to him and started moving us around the dance floor. He was a good dancer and I was impressed. He also smelled delicious and he looked incredibly sexy in his tux. I knew he was uncomfortable in it, but he wore it well. All I wanted to do was rip it off him, one item at a time, before I took my mouth and...oh my. I swallowed loudly and felt myself go damp at the thought of him in my mouth.

Alex braced himself, he was going to ask me something. Something I probably didn't want to hear. "Will you let me make you dinner?" he murmured softly in my ear.

I reared back and searched his face. "What?" I said. "No, we can't *date*." Fuck, what was he doing to me?

"I wasn't asking you on a date. I was asking if you would let me make you dinner. No one at work has to know. I don't think there is anyone at the office that lives in my neighborhood," he said convincingly.

"You want to make me dinner at your place? That sounds like a date to me," I said with a slight frown.

"So, call it a date then," Alex whispered to me. "I am done staying away from you, Cassandra. I can't get you out of my head."

My heart thumped in my chest. I couldn't get him out of my head either. "I don't know," I said, chewing my lip. "We can't date, Alex. We work together. I just promoted you. How would it look?"

"I told you, no one has to know. Just say yes to dinner, Cassandra," he coaxed me as he pulled me closer to him.

I could feel his erection pressing into me, and I wanted to say yes, but if anyone found out, neither one of us would be taken seriously and not to mention my grandfather would kill me.

"Does your girlfriend approve of you propositioning other women while you are on a date with her?" I asked so that I had time to think about what he was saying.

Alex leaned even closer to my ear and said, "She isn't my girlfriend. She's a distraction."

Oh, dear God. I thought my panties were going to melt at that.

"I have somewhere else I have to be," I said to him briskly. "I will think about it."

I stepped back a little bit from him, as we were far too close, and it was attracting some unwanted attention.

Alex stepped back too and murmured, "When will you let me know?"

"Uh, I don't know," I said, flustered under the pressure. "I have to go." I pulled away from him, but he caught my elbow.

"Don't run off."

"I have another engagement," I said. "I will think about what you said and let you know on Monday."

"At the office?" he teased. "Daring."

"Tomorrow then," I snapped.

He chuckled at me and let me go. "I'll be waiting for your call," he said.

I turned on my heel, my full skirt swishing around as I did so, and aimed for the exit. I was just going to slip away.

Rex was waiting for me in a car outside and I had to get to him before I did something really foolish.

~Alex~

SHE LEFT QUICKLY AND QUIETLY. She looked like she was making a run for it and I wondered what could be so important as to pull her away from this event. I found myself following her, keeping my distance as she left the ballroom and hurried quickly across the hotel lobby. Cassandra left the building and I watched her go. A car was waiting for her and as she approached, the back door opened. A masculine hand reached out for her from the inside and helped her in. She gathered her skirts and slid into the seat, closing the door behind her. The car pulled away and I was desperate for tomorrow to come and frustrated that she had sped off into the night with another man. I hoped that douche was her brother or a cousin or something.

I had seen the way she looked at me. Cassandra was as attracted to me as I was to her. It seemed her only concern was because we worked together. It was simple enough to get around. So, we wouldn't get to go to the movies or out to a restaurant, so what? It would be worth it to sneak around with her. In fact, it would probably make it even hotter.

"Hey, there you are," Ella said as she joined me. "I've been looking everywhere for you."

I turned to look at her. Damn. I had forgotten all about her. "Sorry," I said. "Work stuff."

"Oh," she said.

An awkward silence ensued, and I knew I had to end it now that it appeared Cassandra was interested in me. I was no longer interested in second best.

I bit the bullet. "Look, Ella, I don't think this is working," I said as I ran my fingers through my hair.

She looked distraught and I didn't blame her. I had led her on and that wasn't fair. "I'm sorry," I said.

"Yeah, yeah, it's fine," she stammered, but I could see her holding onto her tears. I had nothing else to say to her, so we just stood there not looking at each other for a few minutes.

"I'll go back for my things now if you don't mind?" she finally said, and I nodded. The sooner this was all over, the better.

FIFTEEN

~Cassie~

"Help me," I said as I turned my back to Rex. His fingers pulled down the zipper and the bodice of my gown fell open. I shuffled out of it on the back seat of the limo, thankful that the partition was up, and the driver couldn't see me. Rex watched as I pulled on a tiny, tight, black halter dress which clung to my breasts and barely covered my ass. I swapped my shoes for the same 'porn shoes' I had on the other night. I let my hair down and then turned to him with a smile.

"Perfect," he said huskily, which made me shiver.

He looked perfect too. But then he would look perfect in dirty rags. Tonight, he was a god in his tight, black, leather pants and nothing else, not even shoes. Tonight, he was mine. I pushed all inappropriate thoughts of Alex out of my mind and concentrated on Rex. He was my poison and when he looked at me hungrily, I wanted to crawl into his lap, but refrained with great difficulty. Suddenly, I didn't want to go to the ball. I wanted to go home with him.

"We can turn around," Rex said, somehow reading my thoughts.

I thought about it, and said, "Would you mind?"

He shook his head, but I could see the disappointment on his face.

"No, it's okay," I said. "We'll go."

He smiled at me and compromised by saying, "We'll stay an hour and then I'll take you home."

"Okay," I said, happy with that, and he took my hand.

He cuffed himself to me as the car pulled to a stop. I felt a frisson of nerves as he helped me put on my mask. We got out of the car in an alley around the back of the club that Lachlan had hired for this event. I felt a prickle go down my back as I looked around but didn't see anybody. Since that phone call a few weeks ago, I had been a little bit paranoid. The person had called back a couple of times. I was doing my best to ignore it and just put it down to a prank of some kind, but I never did lose the feeling that I was being watched. It was very unpleasant.

Rex caught my discomfort and pulled me closer to him. It was a dodgy neighborhood, but I felt completely safe with him by my side.

We didn't speak as we entered the club. The loud music washed over us, causing me to go a bit lightheaded. My wide eyes took everybody in and I almost blushed as a woman led a completely naked man past us by a penis leash. I was totally soft-core compared to most of the women in here. I could never imagine treating Rex, or anyone, like that. I cast a quick look at him, and he caught my eye with an amused expression.

"Don't worry, I won't get any ideas," he said with a smirk.

I relaxed a bit. "Have you ever been into any of that?" I asked him, thinking it was something I should already know about him.

He looked surprised that I had asked him a personal question.

He didn't answer for a moment, which made me curious. "No," he said eventually. "Not like that."

I nodded in relief. "Drink?"

"Lead the way, Mistress," he said with a small bow.

I grinned at him. I liked that.

As I fought my way through the throng of people to the bar, I noticed all of the envious stares aimed in our direction. I knew it wasn't because of *me*. Oh no, it was all Rex. The women were practically drooling behind their masks and the men were staring openly at him, wishing they looked like him.

"It's a good thing you are cuffed to me," I shouted into his ear over the thump of the music. "I'm pretty sure I would have lost you on that short walk otherwise."

He looked pleased by my comment but didn't answer me as we were interrupted by Lachlan.

"Hey Sweetcheeks," he yelled at me, slapping my ass and giving me his cheeky smile.

I returned it, taking in his hot bod with an appreciative once-over. He was dressed similar to Rex, but with biker boots on. His short blonde hair was cropped close, and his brown eyes sparkled deliciously at my raking gaze. He was my friend, but I wasn't blind. "Hey, Lach. This is...wow!" I yelled back at him.

He laughed and said, "It is *so* not your thing, baby, but I know why you wanted to come." He cast his glance over Rex and licked his lips. "Hey, Asshole," he sneered.

I looked from Lachlan to Rex in surprise that he had called him that. Rex grimaced at him but didn't say anything. I wondered what all that was about. It was definitely time to find out more about the mystery that was Rex. I had kept my head in the sand for too long, not wanting to know any more than I had to, so I didn't get too attached, and more importantly so that he didn't get too attached to me. There was no future for us in the conventional sense. Rex would never be accepted by my family as a serious suitor. He didn't have old money or even the prospect of making new money. It just seemed best to keep things distant. Lachlan waved us off when our drinks arrived, and I led Rex away to a quieter corner.

~Lachlan~

I WATCHED my best friend lead the man I had a huge crush on away. My jealousy reared its ugly head, but I squashed it for Cassie's sake. For the millionth time, I wished I had never agreed to teach Rex how to be with Cassie. I should have stood my ground and refused. I had hoped that by now he would have reverted to his old form and Cassie would have ditched him, but it didn't seem to be the case. I sighed and turned my back on them. I couldn't bear to see the adoration on his face when he looked at Cassie. Her obliviousness to his affections made me want to slap her, and then kiss her for being the sweet girl that she was. Rex might've been my hot crush, but she was the woman that I loved.

We had met at boarding school. My parents travelled constantly and for stability they had placed me in a co-ed boarding school in England, which was halfway between the States and the Middle East. Cassie's parents just wanted her as far away from them as they could get her. We had become best friends and it had broken both of our hearts when I moved back to New York, leaving Cassie alone.

Even though I knew she only thought of me as a friend, I was, always had been, madly in love with her.

But I wanted Rex so desperately my mouth watered every time I saw him. I knew of his problem and while it clearly wasn't an issue where Cassie was concerned, it had most definitely been in the past. Rex had asked me to help him be what Cassie wanted. I had been reluctant at first as I knew what he was like and he was definitely too depraved for my sweet friend. But he had begged me and said he would do anything. He said that she was his redemption. How can a guy refuse a plea like that? Rex obviously needed redeeming for something, so I said I would help him. I took him on personally and concentrated on getting him to slow down and be gentle with his touch, something he had a hard time grasping. It took time, a lot of it, but he did it and he clearly made Cassie happy or she would have booted him out of the door by now.

But I knew him. Well, as much of him as anyone probably did. Certainly, more so than Cassie did. If Cassie knew his true heart, she would run a mile. I worried about them sometimes, worried that Rex would snap, but seeing them tonight, seeing the way he looked at her, I knew I needn't worry. I was as torn as ever as I cast my eyes over the couple again and my heart pinged when I saw them laughing together. It was the first time I had ever seen him smile and it melted my heart and solidified my resolve to do something about it.

My companion found me moments later and whisked me away to have some fun and to forget my woes.

It almost worked.

~Cassie~

"ASSHOLE?" I asked.

Rex laughed and said, "It's not the nicest nickname, but I probably deserve it."

He kept saying things like that and it made me burn with curiosity about his story. I looked him in the eyes and then over his shoulder with my mouth hanging open. Rex turned as well and coughed before he turned back to me with a smile so wicked it nearly made me drool into my drink.

"Perhaps not such a quiet corner next time," he said, stifling a laugh at my expression.

I couldn't tear my eyes away from the spectacle going on behind Rex. I had watched my fair share of porn, who hadn't? But oh, my lord, I had never been a voyeur to a live sex show before, and a pretty shocking one at that. Well, to me anyway, and I am no prude.

The woman sat on a guy's lap facing outwards being thoroughly serviced in her ass by him. Another naked man was on his knees, lapping away at her clit like an overly enthusiastic puppy. That must be his role, though, because he was indeed attached to his Mistress. She stood by his side and finger fucked the other woman. She was holding the dog leash to which his collar was attached, and not a BDSM collar, but an actual canine type.

"Want to try it?" Rex asked me.

I was shocked until I realized he was joking. "Thanks, but I'll pass," I said with a little laugh, but the thought had been planted. What *would* it be like to have three people attending to my every need? I finished my drink and noticed that Rex had barely touched his. "I'd offer to get you a refill, but you don't need one."

"Not a big drinker," he said and left it at that.

Well, we had come here to be seen and so far, we had just sat in a corner. I decided it was time to show off my man. I dragged him up and led him to the dance floor where people were gyrating around to the hardcore techno. It was a very different setting to the formal elegance of the ball I had left to come here.

"Not a big dancer, either," Rex whispered in my ear.

But I ignored him and pulled him close, moving my hips against his as I brought my uncuffed hand up to rest on his chest. I could feel his heart beating and mine sped up as he moved his free hand up my skirt to rest lightly on my ass.

I felt him get hard as he touched me. He knew I wasn't into public sex shows, that being evident from before, but I wanted him to do something with me right there on the dance floor.

"Touch me," I murmured and pushed his hand to the side of my barely-there thong. I felt him draw in a breath. He moved his fingers up the line of my thong, all the way to the front. I gasped as he brushed past my bare skin. He slid a finger in between my lower lips and over my nub. I held my breath as he slid his finger all the way inside me, pulsed once, twice, and then drew his hand back. His desire showed on his face when he licked his finger, tasting me. My eyes never left his lips as he sucked.

I wanted him so badly.

I whispered, "Time to go," in his ear, brushing my hand lightly over his cock.

I led us out of the club to the waiting car but then I had no idea what to do. Jump him on the back seat or wait until we got home to do our usual thing?

We sat in silence for a while after he uncuffed us. I rubbed my wrist, where a slight bruise was forming on it from being jostled through the crowds, lost in my thoughts. I suddenly felt very uncertain. I had no idea what to do about Rex, or Alex, for that matter. I knew that I wanted to give it a try with Alex, but I also knew it wasn't a good idea. It was all very well trying to keep it a secret, but what if someone found out about us?

I glanced at Rex. He was brooding, glaring out of the window. I was desperately attracted to him. Tonight, was the first time I had seen him relax. We had laughed and talked a bit. I had seen a different side to him, not just as my sexy play partner. I wanted to get to know him better and he was just all kinds of hot.

Was he the safer option? Would I be better off with him? I hardly knew anything about him, and my family would go nuts at me, but we were compatible in the sex department and that was a big thing for me. Plus, he seemed to care about me. I was in a dilemma and didn't know which way to turn: Rex? Alex? Neither? *Both?*

Why couldn't I have my cake and eat it? Why not have the boyfriend that I wanted with Alex and the play time that I craved with Rex? I wondered for the rest of the car ride home if either one of them would agree to such an arrangement. It wouldn't be the first time, and certainly not the last, that two men shared a woman. But would *these* two men?

We arrived back at my building's underground parking and got out of the car. Rex had pulled on a t-shirt on the drive home and I was most disappointed. He threw a coat over me as I was so inappropriately dressed, but luckily it was deserted down here at this time of night.

We rode the private elevator in silence and as we stepped out, I stopped. He bumped into me and I spun around, my thoughts racing. I had come down to two options for the current situation. Alex was left out of the equation for now. I wasn't dating him so what I did here with Rex tonight was nothing to do with him. What mattered now was: bedroom or playroom?

I continued to stare at him as I desperately tried to make up my mind.

"What is it?" Rex asked eventually. "You look like you are about to explode."

Oh, I was about to explode all right. How was I supposed to run a company if I couldn't even decide *that*?

Screw it. It was only me trying to keep my secret sex life separate from my normal life. It should make no difference if I took him to my bed. I grabbed his hand and turned towards my bedroom. My arm jerked painfully as he stopped. I looked back around, and his face was like granite.

~Rex~

"WHAT ARE YOU DOING?" I croaked out.

"Something I should have done before," she said carefully.

I felt like I was going to pass out. I shook my head and stayed where I was, even when she tugged on me.

"Cassandra, no," I said more firmly. "You don't want to take me in there."

Oh God, my heart was hammering. I wanted to go in there with her more than anything. I had waited for this moment, but I kept seeing her pristine, white bed marred by my darkness.

"Why not?" she asked quietly.

I couldn't tell her the truth. That I had been forced into teenage prostitution by my own mother and her pimp and that I'd eventually murdered them in their sleep and now I killed people for a living.

How could I say any of that? She would run a mile, and so she should. I was fooling myself to think I deserved her. There was nothing in my cover story that would put her off me in that way. I had created it so when she asked, I came across as normal, not as some psycho mother-killer who shot people in the head for a living and walked away a richer man. I stayed silent and she tugged on me again.

"I-I need to go," I stammered and pulled my hand from hers.

"Rex, no. I don't want you to go. We can go the other way," she said, stepping forward as I backed away from her.

"No, not tonight," I said.

I made it into the elevator. My body was fighting with my brain to not leap back out and drag her by her hair to the pure, angelic bed and have my disgusting, evil way with her. I clenched my fists and closed my eyes, drawing in a deep breath.

"I will see you on Tuesday," I whispered as I punched the elevator button and the doors closed.

All of my old feelings, that I thought I had suppressed were flooding back in the face of her decision, and if I stayed, I would hurt her. I huddled into the corner and sank to the floor. Then I did something that I hadn't done in over a decade.

I wept.

SIXTEEN

~Alex~

I was climbing the walls. After I said goodbye to Ella, and she left with her belongings, I started to pace. I kept checking my phone to see if Cassandra had messaged, or called, or emailed, but it was radio silence. She was probably still at whatever it was that had pulled her away from the ball.

I kept replaying it in my head. Dancing with her, flirting with her, her seductive smile and mischievous, green eyes. She was perfection.

I groaned out loud and poured myself a drink. Then another after that and I resumed pacing.

At 3 A.M., when there was still nothing, I went to bed. She wouldn't call me at this time of the morning, but I wanted to be up early so I could wait. 'Lame' didn't even cover it, but I didn't care. All I wanted was that phone call.

~Cassie~

I WAS GOING CRAZY. Rex had run away from me, literally! I was so confused. Why had he acted so strangely? Maybe I had read him all wrong and he didn't want more from me except a bi-weekly play session. He had been so adamant that I shouldn't take him into my bedroom. But why? That question kept bouncing around my head, driving me more and more crazy.

I eventually stopped pacing like a caged animal when I saw the blinking light on my answering machine. I really did not want to play that back. I would deal with it tomorrow and if it was that creepy caller, I would call the police. In the meanwhile, I checked the door to make sure it was bolted again and, flicking the key to lock the elevator, I flounced off to my bedroom. I collapsed naked on the bed after ripping off my clothes, not very happy to be in there alone when there were *two* men out there that I wanted.

A decision had to be made. I had to stop being so indecisive. I eventually made it with a sigh and climbed into bed with it weighing heavily on my mind.

~Rex~

I DIDN'T KNOW how long I stayed in the elevator, crouched in the corner. I knew my legs were stiff, though, so it was probably a while. I straightened up painfully and shook my legs out. What had I been thinking? I should have let her take me wherever the fuck she'd wanted to go. It could have been a corner in our relationship.

I had gotten my sadistic feelings under control and before I changed my mind, punched the button for the elevator to go back up so I could devour her and tell her how I felt about her, but I didn't go anywhere. I frowned and tried again, flashing the card twice before I gave up. Cassandra must have locked it from upstairs. She never did that. My thoughts went back to the person I had seen watching her a few weeks ago. I hadn't seen him since. I watched her on the monitors at home, she seemed fine and no one had entered that shouldn't have been there. I worried that something had happened to her while I was having my breakdown, but then my paranoid brain went to the obvious reason. She had done it so that *I* couldn't get back up.

She had locked me out.

That thought hit me hard and my fists clenched again. I nearly snapped the key card in my anger; it was digging into my palm, cutting me, but I didn't care. I had fucked up and now I had lost her.

No! I couldn't lose her; she was my angel. My only chance at redemption. She was the only woman I could love and treat well. I wanted her to love me back, even for a little bit, so I knew that I wasn't completely lost to the pit.

And she had tried. Her actions had screamed it, and I had freaked and bailed like the fucking idiot I was. Furious with myself, I walked over to the Mustang I'd left there earlier and grabbed the keys off the back tire. I needed a release in a controlled environment, or I was going to end up hurting an innocent woman.

I had been innocent once, I remembered briefly. But I had caused enough harm already without adding to it. I headed to Lachlan's club. It was the only place I could find refuge. It would still be open, even though he was at the ball.

MINUTES LATER, I knocked on the door of the club. The peephole slid open and then slammed shut. The door flew open a second after, startling me. Lachlan stood there looking like he wanted to kill me.

"You!" he snarled. "You had better walk away and not darken my door again." He started to slam the door shut but I practically punched it off its hinges to stop him.

"Asshole," he warned me, "you make one wrong move and I have five guys here who have been dying to take you down."

"It'll take more than five with the mood I'm in," I growled at him, knowing he wouldn't lay a finger on me. It wasn't his style, however Lach knew me and I didn't scare him. He should be afraid, but he didn't stand for that shit. He was deadly serious about the security. It gave me pause.

"Mood or not, you had better leave," he said, crossing his arms with a wicked smile. "Or I will call Cassie right now and tell her that not only are you here, but also *why* you are here."

Cassie, Cassie, Cassandra. My perfect princess. God, what was I doing here? I slumped in the doorway. Lachlan dropped his defensive stance and took pity on me. He took me by the arm and said, "One drink, no play, and you tell me what's up. That's the deal, or you can leave."

I wanted the drink. I didn't want to play anymore, and I didn't want to talk either.

Lachlan dragged me over to a table near the bar and ordered me a Scotch. I downed it in one gulp, and he let me have another. He knew I wouldn't talk without it. He tapped his fingers on the table and waited. After one more, I was feeling kind of tipsy.

That's when he asked me, "Why did you come here tonight?"

I looked up at him, having forgotten he was even there. "Because I'm an asshole," I said.

"Tell me something I don't know," Lachlan said wryly.

I glared at him. He glared back and I looked away.

"I don't deserve her," I said suddenly.

"Why not?" he asked. He wasn't going to coddle me, and I knew it.

"All the innocents, it's wrong. I'm wrong," I said. I was starting to slur as I sloshed the Scotch around the glass.

"What innocents?" he asked.

I looked at him blankly and leaned over to put my cheek on the granite tabletop. Three doubles and I was practically out for the count.

"The targets," I slurred and closed my eyes. Somewhere in the back of my head I knew to shut up. That was why it wasn't good to drink in my line of work. Loose lips sink ships and will send me straight to prison for the rest of my life, or worse.

"Nuthin'," I said and closed my eyes.

~Lachlan~

I SIGHED. I didn't see him going anywhere anytime soon. The man looked exhausted and maybe a few drinks would help him sleep. I had a room where he could crash for the night.

"Rex," I said as I nudged his shoulder.

He sat upright suddenly, his eyes flying open. "Wha...?"

"You can crash here tonight," I said.

He looked at me through blurry eyes. "With you?" he asked with such a wicked laugh it made my heart thud.

Oh, fuck I wanted that, too bad he was joking. "You wish, Asshole," I sneered to cover up the growing desire. "By yourself," I added firmly, in case he got any ideas about taking one of my girls while I wasn't looking. I indicated to two of the security guys and told them to take him to a side room. They picked him up and, standing on either side of him, helped him stagger towards the waiting bed. They shoved him down and he crawled into a ball and fell asleep.

I stayed with him for a while, watching him. I wanted to crawl up onto the bed and hold him. He looked so lost, even in sleep. Whatever his problems were, they were deep, and they were painful. He seemed to believe that Cassie was the only one who could help him. If only he knew that I could also steer him towards some happiness. If he would just let me. I knew then that I had to have a conversation with Cassie. It had been a long time coming, and the sooner I had the balls to do it, the better for all of us. I just hoped she would listen, take it on board and agree to my proposal. It was a long shot, but one I had to take for my own sanity, as well as Rex's by the looks of it.

AFTER A FEW MORE HOURS HAD PASSED, I closed up and headed out. I doubted Rex would be up anytime soon, so I went home to shower and change. After a couple of hours of sleep, I went back to the club with coffee and bagels.

As expected, Rex was still sleeping. Well, passed out. He didn't look like he was resting very much. The sheets were all tangled around him and he looked tormented. I shoved my hands into the pockets of my jeans and watched him again. He really was the finest looking man alive.

I turned and went to my office to wait for him. I had work to do that would keep me occupied.

Only moments later, I looked up and saw Rex standing in the doorway. He just stared at me for a few minutes.

"Sorry about last night," he mumbled. "I didn't do anything, uhm, inappropriate, did I?"

He seemed genuinely concerned that he had acted badly and looked relieved when I shook my head with a chuckle. "No. But, man, you are a lightweight! I don't think I have ever seen anyone get that wasted that quickly on a couple of Scotches."

He grimaced at me and it made me laugh even more.

"I'm not a big drinker," he said.

"You aren't big on anything," I retorted.

He looked startled before he threw me a gorgeous half-smile. Holy hell, the man was divine.

"I should get going," he mumbled and turned to go. "Uh, thanks for last night, you know, not letting me do anything stupid, and also for not telling Cassandra."

"Anytime, Asshole," I said. I had no intention of mentioning this to Cassie. It would make her walk and that wasn't something I wanted. I crossed my arms and watched him slink away with his tail between his legs.

SEVENTEEN

~Alex~

Sunday afternoon had come and practically gone. I wasn't so confident that Cassandra would call me. I had waited by the phone all day, like a fucking loser, not even wanting to leave the apartment in case I lost my signal while she tried to contact me.

I jumped a mile when there was a loud, persistent knocking on the door. It was unusual, as visitors had to be buzzed up, so I glared through the peephole, but all I saw was a huge, white, floppy hat.

Curiosity getting the better of me, I pulled the door open and Cassandra looked up at me from under the hat, also decked out in big, round sunglasses with an anxious look on her face.

"Uh, hi," I said.

"Can I come in?" she blurted out, gripping the handle of her oversized purse tight against her shoulder.

"Yeah, yeah, of course," I said, stepping back and letting her pass. She raced in and then relaxed a bit when I closed the door. I leaned back against it and regarded her. She seemed nervous. I was too. Was she here to tell me to go to hell or the opposite? I had no doubt though that she was heaven, in every which way.

She took off her big hat and sunglasses and threw them onto the couch. Then she just stared at me. I stared back and waited for whatever it was she had to say.

"Hi," she said eventually with a soft smile.

"Hey," I replied with what I hoped was a sexy smile back. "Can I get you anything?" I indicated to the kitchen.

She shook her head. "Alex, can we really do this? Can we really see each other in secret?"

"Yes," I said instantly, straightening up from the door and stepping closer to her. "We don't need to go out. I am an excellent cook and have all the latest movies out on Blu-ray. We could hole up here indefinitely." I grinned at her and she returned it.

"Okay then. I'm in," she said.

I leapt over the back of the couch to take her in my arms and kiss her, but she put a hand up to stop me to my crushing disappointment.

"Wait, we need ground rules," she said and continued without waiting for an answer. "One, we meet here most of the time, every now and again you can come to my place for a change of scenery. Two, we do not look at each other if we see each other at work. Three, add my number to your phone under my middle name, Ruby, and I will add you to mine as Peter." She shoved a crumpled piece of paper at me. It was her number. I raised my eyebrow that she knew my middle name, but then again, she also knew where I lived. Perks of being my boss.

"Four," she continued at my silence, "I am going to have to carry on seeing other men every now and again, for dates only, to be seen out in public with the male species. The rumor mill is too fierce on the Upper East Side. And five, get over here and kiss me now!"

I didn't need to be asked twice after that and was on her like a fly to honey. Her lips were as soft as silk and she tasted minty fresh. I was acutely aware at this point that I probably tasted like coffee, but I didn't care, I just wanted to keep on kissing her.

Cassandra pulled away and asked, "Do you agree to the rules?"

"Yes," I said. "Although, when you said, 'dates only,' does that mean you want to be exclusive to me in the bedroom sense?" I added slyly to cover up my nerves in case her answer wasn't what I wanted to hear.

She flushed prettily and it increased my smile. "I have to keep up appearances," she stammered.

I linked my hands around the back of her neck and kissed her again. "Do you want to be my secret girlfriend, Cassandra?" I whispered against her lips.

"Yes," she whispered back, pushing herself into me.

Her soft breasts pressed against me and I wanted to rip her clothes off her, which was suddenly completely doused by a very unpleasant thought. I only had Ella's word to go on that she was safe. She had told me, after I had asked, that she was clean, but I had always been careful up to that point. I always wore a condom, from the day I lost my virginity in college, so that I knew *I* was okay.

I didn't want to risk going anywhere near Cassandra until I knew for sure.

I stepped back and she looked up at me with those

incredible green eyes. "Do you want to be my secret boyfriend, Alex?" she asked, licking her lips slightly.

"Oh, God, yes," I said, not caring that I sounded like a desperate fool. I kissed her again but this time *she* stepped back.

She smiled hesitantly and said, "I have to go, I have this family thing." She waved her hand about almost nervously.

"Okay," I said. "I guess I will see you tomorrow at work then. Or not," I amended at her look. "Although, it might look suspicious if we don't ever look at each other. Maybe a cursory eye meet, and a cool nod might be more fitting?" I suggested with a slight laugh.

She giggled and it sent a rocket of lust shooting through my entire body. "Excellent suggestion," she said. "But it will be difficult to look at you and not think of all the things I want to do with you," she added wickedly.

I nearly whisked her off to my bedroom right then, safety be damned. "It will be difficult for me to look at you and not imagine where and what those other tattoos are that you've got hiding," I murmured.

She smiled enigmatically at me. "You will just have to wait and see," she said.

Leaning over, I gave her a quick peck on the lips. She grabbed her hat and glasses and made as quick an exit as she did entrance. I was over the moon that she had come to me and didn't care about the secrecy. Better that I will never have to meet her family and be judged by her parents, or worse, her grandparents, for being from the wrong side of the tracks. And better still that she will never meet my family and judged them. Not that I would ever introduce anyone I was dating to my family. Well, my mother and sister, anyways. My dad had left when I was still a kid and I never saw him again. I had clawed my way out of that hell hole and had no intention of going back near it.

I realized that we'd parted without setting a date for us to meet here again. I knew it would probably only be on the weekend again, so I messaged "Ruby" to ask her to dinner at my apartment on Friday at 7 P.M. and also asked how she liked her eggs.

EIGHTEEN

~Cassie~

My phone buzzed as I made my way back to the waiting car. Probably not the best idea to bring my driver here. I would have to find an alternative means of transportation. I checked it and it was "Peter." I smiled and opened the message. Then I frowned. Shit, Friday? What was I going to tell him and what was I going to do about Rex? I quickly messaged back that I had an engagement on Friday but would be there Saturday at 5 P.M. and liked my eggs any way he chose to deliver them to me in bed.

A thrill went through me as I thought about spending the night with him. A message came back that read: "5 P.M. suits me and I will make scrambled so I can eat them off you."

I giggled in surprise and delight and sent one back saying: "Only if I get to eat some too..."

He came back with: "Of course, I'm not greedy."

Oh God, I couldn't wait until Saturday. It seemed like a lifetime away, but it was good to wait, I decided. I had wanted him to take me back in his apartment a few moments ago but I knew I had Rex to deal with. Things seemed different with Alex and I didn't know what I wanted to do about Rex yet. I didn't want to lose him completely. He gave me everything I needed. I had no idea if Alex could. Or would, even. It wasn't everyone's cup of tea, even though what I liked was nothing compared to the extremes that some people went to. Most people liked it straight up, plain and simple. *I* wasn't one of them, even though I enjoyed regular sex, and I was damn sure I would enjoy regular sex with Alex, but I needed that edge, that thrill. I faltered in my decision. I knew deep down that if Rex hadn't run away from me last night, I wouldn't have come here today. A relationship with Alex was risky and it was going to be difficult, it didn't matter how much I wanted him. I would have pursued a deeper relationship with Rex had he wanted that. The man clearly had issues, but then who didn't? Ah, hell. What's done was done. The only thing for it was to avoid sleeping with Rex, until I knew what I really wanted.

I'm such a bitch. But that thought did nothing to change my mind.

~Alex~

I WENT to my laptop and checked what time the free clinic, that was on the way to work, opened on Mondays. I was relieved to see it opened at 8:30 so if I got there as it opened, I should be able to get in and out and up to work on time. I couldn't believe I didn't think about doing this sooner. I just hoped that I got the results back by Saturday at 5 P.M. God, it was practically a whole week away. I was probably going to have to go back to my nightly ritual at this rate. I ran my hands through my hair in frustration but decided it would be worth the wait.

I GOT up a bit early on Monday morning so I could make it to the clinic as it opened. Luck was on my side and I was early. There was no one else waiting outside. I was embarrassed to be standing out there, but it had to be done. I was flicking through my emails as I stood there and with a quick glance up, I came face to face with that guy, Rex, from the gym. Oh, for fuck's sake. Now it was *really* embarrassing. I had hoped I wouldn't run into anyone I knew. Now, we would each know we had been there the next time we saw each other at the gym.

Rex grimaced at me and nodded briskly as the woman, thankfully, opened the door. We both rushed inside.

I got to the reception first and told them why I was there in hushed tones. The nurse gave me some forms to fill out and then smiled at Rex and said, "Hey there, we've been expecting you." She flashed her files at him and gestured for him to follow her. He went off as my phone rang on the counter where I'd left it. I picked it up, distractedly. Christ, that guy is a regular? Didn't the man know how to be protected? There again, the skanks he probably hooked up with no doubt preferred him au natural.

I glanced at the screen and smiled. "Hey beautiful," I said into the phone. "How is my lovely Ruby this morning?"

I saw Rex glance back over his shoulder at me as I went to sit down to fill out my forms.

"Just perfect," Cassie replied with a chuckle. "You?" She sounded like she was struggling with something and then I heard a whispered voice.

"Yeah, good. Everything okay there?" I asked in concern.

"Uh, yes, just trying to do ten things at once, you know..."

"Well, slow down, I don't want you worn out by Saturday," I said in a low, husky voice and heard her catch her breath.

"In that case," she murmured, "I will call in sick and rest up all week."

"If you do that then there is no reason to wait until Saturday," I pointed out as I finished filling out my details and handed the forms back to the receptionist. Good thing I knew how to multi-task, the place was filling up now.

"Mmm," she said, "I am liking this idea more and more."

The nurse caught my attention, so I said quickly, "Sorry, baby, I've got to go. I will catch up with you in a bit." Gee, that didn't sound suspicious at all.

"Okay," she said. "I've got to dash as well."

We hung up and I dutifully followed the nurse, eager to get that personal humiliation over with as quickly as possible.

~Rex~

I WAS suspicious about the phone call that Alex guy took. I was probably being paranoid, but I knew Cassandra's middle name was Ruby, after her grandmother. There were very few facts about her that I didn't know. I had been watching but hadn't seen her bring anyone back to her apartment, so it was probably just a coincidence. Much like the fact that Alex and I kept running into each other. I wasn't impressed to be seen here by him. I knew that the guy already thought I was some kind of weird sex fiend and this would only fan that fire. Although, why I cared, I didn't know. There was something I couldn't put my finger on about him. I determined it was maybe time to do a bit of digging on Alex, whatever his last name was. Wouldn't be too hard to find out from the gym records. Might be time to see if this guy was for real or some kind of professional tailing me.

I sat back and let the nurse do her thing. This was so completely pointless, but Cassandra had insisted on regular testing and it was the 1st of the month, so here I was. God knows what the nurses must have thought of me. Not that I cared, but it would be interesting, nonetheless. However, I came back clean every time because the only woman I was ever with was Cassandra. It was a physical impossibility for me to be with anyone else, not that I wanted to anyway. I thought I had managed to deter most of her lovers or poten-tial lovers, but I assumed a few of them had fallen through the cracks at one point or another.

Well definitely one, maybe two at the most, and now I was watching her all the time so I could ensure she stayed safe. My cameras were set up to record, so I could go back home and rewind to where I left off. I could watch her get ready for work and I knew her personal doctor would be over to see to her testing. I loved studying her when she was so unaware that I was watching her every move because she was so natural and at ease.

The nurse finished up and I left at the same time Alex left his room. We nodded awkwardly at each other and I could tell this guy was a first timer. He looked seriously uncomfortable and was eyeing up the waiting room like it was about to bite his ass. Decked out in his fairly expensive suit with his fancy haircut, he looked so out of place it would have made me laugh if I were so inclined to be amused by anyone else's business, which I wasn't. We parted ways with grim looks as my burner cell rang, and we headed off in different directions.

I WATCHED on the screen as I drank a cup of coffee. The Barbie-doll type housekeeper was rifling through Cassandra's things. Pawing through her drawers and rifling through her closet. She pulled out a pink dress that Cassandra had on the Saturday night of the ball before she changed. I watched with interest as she stripped off naked. I barely noticed her body, I had absolutely no interest in her as a woman. She tried the dress on and got annoyed that it kept slipping down at the top. I smiled into my cup. Cassandra's breasts were magnificent. The woman twirled again, unaware that she was being watched. I wasn't concerned. She had a right to be there, I'd had her vetted already along with every other employee who worked in the building. I just found it interesting to see the jealousy on her face. It changed into something slightly more sinister, and that caught my attention. Perhaps there was more to this woman than met the eye. I made a mental note to keep my eye on her.

MY PHONE BUZZED and I glared at it with open hatred. Seemed my plans had changed, and I wasn't in the best of moods about it. In fact, I was pissed off and that was not a good thing. I had started to wish that I hadn't taken this job. I had decided to do it for personal reasons and that was just plain stupid. The Captain had called me as I left the clinic this morning and told me to get my ass to England. The target had flown the coop and I was expected to follow. Not that it usually bothered me. I had traveled all over with my job, I was a ghost, in and out and back home. Sorted.

However, I didn't want to leave Cassandra now. I was desperate to see her after running away from her on Saturday night. I needed to see her, but I didn't know how to ask her for time outside of our arrangement. I had tried to push the trip back until Wednesday so I could go to her on Tuesday night as normal, but the Captain was adamant I had to leave tonight. I had received an envelope with additional directives, and it was pretty standard. I'd be gone a couple of days, but it was a couple of days too many.

The Captain had set up a meeting with an arms dealer for what I needed, and while I would have preferred the use of my own weapon, it was impossible on international jobs.

In the end, I messaged Cassandra to tell her I was traveling for business, leaving that night. If she wanted to see me, then she would tell me.

She messaged me back that she was disappointed but made no mention of seeing me until I got back. I knew I had fucked up by leaving her the way I had and now I was paying the price.

NINETEEN

~Alex~

I made it to work with a few seconds to spare. Rick came hovering but I really couldn't be bothered with my friend right now.

Man, the job was killer, coupled with the fact that my head wasn't in the game. I had to get my shit sorted out. I didn't work this hard to let it all go to crap now, over a woman no less.

I spent the rest of the day with my head down and my door closed. Cassandra had messaged a couple of times, but that had been the only time I looked away from my work.

AS I PACKED up for the day, I thought it had gone well. Much better. I didn't need to be acting like a lovesick schmuck, especially now that I had got the girl.

The girl in question was in the crowded elevator as I stepped in and after our agreed-upon cursory nod, I ignored her. My phone beeped in my pocket. I took it out and glanced down to read it. It made my heart thump. She had messaged me from inches away saying she wished we were alone so I could lift her skirt up and feel how wet she was for me. I had to shuffle and move my briefcase in front of me when she sent another one saying she was desperate to go down on me.

Shit, she was a wicked woman. Didn't she know what she was doing to me here? Fortunately, everyone else was on their phones after the end of the workday and didn't even notice us. So, I messaged her back, playing along, although I had never engaged in "sexting" before, saying that I couldn't wait to have her tongue wrapped around my dick. I heard her clear her throat and she shuffled a bit further away from me. I smiled to myself, glad to have rattled her cage as much as she had mine.

My happy mood was completely doused when my phone rang, and I recognized the Jersey area code. I hadn't spoken to my mother in years and had no intention of starting now. I ignored the call as the elevator doors opened and I exited with everyone else. Cassandra sent me another message as she got into her car, asking if everything was okay since she had seen me frown when I ignored the call.

She was the sweetest creature on the planet to have noticed and cared. I called her as the car was already on its way and I was left far behind on the sidewalk.

"Nothing for you to worry about," I said as soon as she answered.

"That sounds ominous," she replied.

"Family shit. You know." I shrugged.

"Ah, yes, family shit. I have a big stinking pile of that, so no worries. I understand," she said, and I laughed.

"You are perfect," I said. "Has anyone ever told you that?"

"Maybe once or twice," she teased. "You can say it again if you like."

"Perfect," I said, and she made that delicious giggling sound that drove me to distraction. "Get your driver to drop you off at my place," I said suddenly.

"Not on a school night," she chided. "Besides, I want to make you wait. I want you so hard that when I *do* wrap my tongue around your dick, you won't be able to hold back."

I groaned out loud. "Fuck's sake, woman. You are going to be so in for it on Saturday, I hope you are prepared."

Her delighted laugh came down the phone. "That's what I'm counting on, bye-bye now." She hung up on me and I knew the shower was beckoning me when I got home.

~Lachlan~

I HAD FINALLY CONNECTED the dots. I had been working on this project for weeks in secret and now I finally had the truth. I knew who he was and what he did. I didn't care. I still wanted to be with him. I knew Cassie would have a problem with it, though. It would have to be something that remained under wraps. I would have to confront him and let him know that his secret was safe with me. Stuffing the pieces of paper back into the folder, I tapped it on the desk to straighten it. I gripped it tightly and then spun in my chair to unlock the safe. I placed it in carefully and then closed the door quietly, locking away the information from the rest of the world. I had no idea when to confront him. He was going to flip his lid when I told him I knew. I needed more time to think about it. But not too much. I had plans to speak to Cassie about our relationship soon, and it would be better if Rex was informed of my knowledge *before,* I made her broach the subject with him.

"Lach?" my companion called through the closed door. "Are you ready to get out of here? I want to take you home and have you tie me up."

"Absolutely, Captain," I said and smiled at him as he opened the door. He so wasn't my type, but if it weren't for him, I never would have found out the truth about Rex, so taking one for the team was a necessity.

TWENTY

~Cassie~

I hated to admit that I was quite relieved to get Rex's message that he was going out of town. I was a coward, but it saved me from having to worry about our relationship, or whatever it was, until he got back. I was free to look forward to my date with Alex for now. I hadn't been able to resist sending those messages in the elevator. He had looked so hot in his three-piece suit that matched his dark blue eyes perfectly. I curled up on the sofa with my glass of red wine and reread what he had sent back with a grin. I hoped that he would be into a bit of play because I really wanted to tie him up and tease him into submission.

But that was something that would come later, it defi-nitely was not an opener if you had no idea what the other person was into.

I messaged him: "Can't wait to be with you."

I really had wanted to go to his place tonight, but I had

a call coming through from my grandfather in about half an hour, from somewhere on his travels, that I just couldn't miss. I knew he was checking up on me, under the pretense of a social call, but I didn't mind. It must be hard for him to let go of the reins he'd held so tightly for so long.

Alex messaged back: "Me either. This is dragging by..."

I smiled, feeling good about the decision for the first time since I made it.

~Alex~

THE WEEK DRAGGED on for me. Saturday seemed light-years away and I was anxious because the clinic still hadn't called me back. I closed my office door on the morning before the big date and made a quick call to them asking if they had my results back. Their response was that they had been unusually busy and short staffed, and it was taking longer than normal. I grimaced, but whatever. I was stopping at the drugstore on the way home anyway as I was Alex Monaghan, sexual safety freak (usually), and Cassandra struck me as the type of girl who would insist on being safe. Plus, there was no way that I wasn't taking her to my bed tomorrow.

SATURDAY NIGHT FINALLY ARRIVED. I was making chicken piccata and pasta. Cassie was responsible for the wine. I couldn't wait to see her. She turned up promptly at 5 P.M. and I let her in.

She was dressed in a casual summer dress that showed off her killer body. She handed me the wine. "Wow, that smells delicious."

"Told you I was a good cook," I replied, taking the wine and opening it. I had no idea if it was any good, I knew nothing about wine, but assumed it was one of her favorites.

"Yes, you did," she murmured as she took in her surroundings as if seeing them for the first time.

"Please, sit," I said, indicating the couch with the wine glass before I handed it to her.

"This is a nice apartment," she said, as she sat.

"I am sure it has nothing on yours," I said with a smile that she returned.

"Well, the Bellingham's don't do things by half," she said and laughed. "My grandparents gave it to me. I would have chosen something a little less..."

"Less what?" I asked as she trailed off.

"Just a little less," she said and laughed again.

I settled Cassandra at the dining table, and we ate and chatted, learning things about each other. I was glad that we had some things in common aside from a mutual, heated attraction. We steered clear of family conversation and that suited both of us just fine. We finished up and we both knew the moment was upon us. We glanced at each other and Cassie chewed her lip. I just couldn't keep my hands off her then. I dove at her, pulling her to me. She responded in kind, bringing her hands up to undo my shirt. I walked her back into the bedroom, and she kicked off her shoes. She stepped back from me and seductively started to undo the buttons on the front of her dress. I reached for her, wanting to do it myself, but she shook her head and pouted at me.

"Don't you want to see where the other tattoos are?"

My mouth watered. I nodded; my eyes fixed firmly on hers. She slowly, slowly carried on undoing the buttons. I was practically salivating when she had reached the final button at her waist and nothing had yet been revealed. She peeled the top of her dress away to expose her breasts and I moaned.

Oh my God. My whole body responded to her inked nipples. I leaned forward to trace my finger around one of the daisy chains. She threw her head back as I touched her.

"Fuck me," I whispered. "You are beautiful."

I lowered my mouth to her, needing to follow the trace of my finger with my tongue. She clutched the back of my head as I sucked her nipple into my mouth, suckling on her urgently. She pulled away and continued to undress me. My cock sprung free the second my jeans were undone. She turned and shimmied out of her panties and crawled onto my bed. I didn't need any persuading to follow her and was soon kissing her like my life depended on it.

"Oh, Cassandra," I murmured against her lips.

"Call me Cassie," she whispered back.

I looked up, startled, and then laughed.

"Yes, just as pretty," I said before I took to her breasts again, filling my mouth with her nipple. I wanted to stay there forever, but I also wanted to taste her. I moved my mouth down her body and pushed her legs apart. She was bare there and I could see her clit glistening. I touched her lightly and it sent a shiver over her. She cried out and pushed herself against my fingers. Encouraged, I slipped my fingers inside her. Fuck, she was so wet. I shuffled down the bed. My lips met her clit and I flicked my tongue over her., She came suddenly, pulsing around my fingers. I wanted her to do it again, so I continued my licking, sucking, and stroking. I got my wish moments later and smiled against her as she writhed against my lips.

"Oh, Alex," she said, breathless. "I want you, now." Her commanding tone had me chuckling.

"Yes, ma'am," I said and leaned over to the nightstand where I had already stashed my jumbo box of condoms. I intended to go through as many of them as I could. Her eyes followed me, and she flicked them briefly to the foil packet and then back up to my eyes.

She sat up and took it from me. "Allow me," she said and ripped it open.

"Uh," I muttered. I had never had a woman put one on me before but relinquished the control to her as she gently rolled it over my cock. I twitched against her touch and I almost came on the spot when she made an "mmmmm" sound in the back of her throat. She moved her hands up, tracing the grooves of my solid six-pack, and up over my pecs to the back of my neck. She pulled me down on top of her and wrapped her legs around me. Not even the world ending could have stopped me. I had no choice but to enter her. I pushed against her and she yielded with a soft moan, sheathing me completely. I kissed her as I thrust even further into her. She met me in a perfect rhythm that had me breaking into a sweat. I was holding out for her orgasm, but I was ready to burst. I palmed her breasts and kissed her, wrapping my arms tightly around her to bring us closer together. I felt the first waves of her orgasm rip through her. With a loud cry of my own, I let myself go, pushing down on her hips with my hands to get as far into her as I could.

I was breathing heavily when I rolled off her and discarded the condom quickly into the wastepaper basket. Then I was back next to her, holding her close as our breathing steadied.

"You set the bar quite high, Mr. Monaghan," she said with a smile. "A girl could get used to that."

"We've only just started, Ms. Bellingham," I replied glibly. "You ain't seen nothing yet."

She burst out laughing and rolled on top of me. "Oh really?" she asked, sitting up and straddling me. "Do your worst," she dared and with the challenge accepted, we proceeded to work our way through the box in the nightstand.

TWENTY-ONE

~Cassie~

I awoke to Alex watching me. I was pleasantly stiff as I stretched and smiled at him.

"Morning," I said.

"Is it?" he asked with a comically confused look. "Time seems to have lost all meaning."

"It had better be morning," I replied. "You promised me breakfast in bed."

"Ah, that I did," he said. "Scrambled eggs, if I recall?"

"Mm," I replied, snuggling further into the bed. "So we could eat them off each other."

"How about we start with coffee?" he said and got up to pull his jeans on. He left them undone, showing off his gorgeous "V" shape and, had I not already been lying down, I would have swooned.

"Alex?" I asked before he left the bedroom.

"Yeah?" He turned back around.

I indicated the nightstand. "Just so you know, we don't need those from my side." I said it casually, but it had a flush going over his cheeks and he cleared his throat, shuffling uncomfortably.

"I, uh, I..." he stammered.

I raised my eyebrow at him and sat up, wanting a response. He tried again and came to sit next to me.

"Before you agreed to go out with me, I had a relationship that may have started out quite irresponsibly," he stated, forcing himself to look into my eyes. "I am just taking precautions, until I know I am, uh, you know."

"Okay," I said. "You don't need to be embarrassed, Alex. Thank you for telling me, and for being so responsible."

He looked up sharply at my tone. I was teasing him! I bit my lip so as not to laugh and asked, "Was it with the distraction?"

He laughed as well. "Yes, yes it was."

I nodded and let him go to make coffee. He had only been gone a few minutes when I decided to join him. I pulled on his discarded shirt and did up a few of the buttons. I fluffed out my hair and went in search of him. I found him in the kitchen with his back turned towards me, flicking through his phone. I walked over to him. He raised his eyes and his mouth dropped open.

"I hope you don't mind," I said, smoothing down his shirt.

"Mind?" he asked. "Oh no, I don't mind. In fact, I think that is the only thing you should wear, ever."

I lowered my eyes flirtatiously and twirled my hair round my finger. "Does that mean I get to take it home with me?"

He threw his phone onto the counter and crossed over to me. He gathered me to him, his hands in my hair. "You aren't going home," he murmured. "I don't get to touch, kiss or even look at you during the week. You are staying right here all weekend so I can have my fill of you before the week starts again." He turned me around and bent me over the back of the sofa, lifting the shirt up over my hips. My breathing got deeper. I was highly aroused as he grabbed my ass. Then I heard him say, "Fuck," and back away.

I spun around. "What?"

"I need a...fuck," he said again and turned back to the kitchen with clenched fists. "That would have been so fucking hot," he said mostly to himself.

My disappointment was profound. Yeah, that would have been fucking hot. I crossed my legs feeling the dampness between my thighs. I made a decision and headed back to the bedroom. I opened the nightstand and pulled out the box. I left one in the drawer and then went back into the sitting room. He watched me as I carefully began taking the remaining condoms out of the box and placing them strategically around the apartment. One on the dining table, one on the coffee table, one on the sideboard, and so on until I leaned over and placed one on the back of the sofa. He stifled his laugh of delight at my actions. I held up the last one in between my index and middle fingers and stalked slowly towards him. "This one goes in here," I said, slipping it into the front pocket of his jeans. His cock went rigid again and without a word, he lifted me onto the kitchen counter, this time ready to see his actions through to the end.

TWENTY-TWO

~Alex~

I lay in bed on Sunday night and I missed her. She had gone home a couple of hours ago. As if she knew I was thinking about her, my phone rang next to me.

"Hi, Princess," I said with a smile.

There was a pause. "Princess?" she asked.

"Yeah, that dress you had on at the ball...you looked like a fairy-tale princess," I admitted shyly.

She snickered and said, "That would make you my fairy-tale prince."

"I can live with that," I said. "Even if it means I have to wear those fancy-ass breeches and knee-high boots."

"Ah, but you get to carry a sword and ride on a white horse," she pointed out.

"I am liking this more and more. Although, does it mean I have to rescue you from your prison tower?"

"Would you?" she asked coquettishly.

"But of course!" I said gallantly.

"No one has ever given me a pet name before," she said quietly.

"Really?" I asked. "Never?"

"No, well except for Lachlan, but I don't suppose he counts," Cassie said.

"Who is Lachlan?" I asked, settling back and relaxing.

"My best friend. We went to school together," she said.

"Where *did* you go to school?" I asked curiously.

"England and Switzerland and then college back in England," she said.

"Oh," I said, feeling completely unsophisticated after that revelation. I had never left the States. "Ah," I said then, "I get it now."

"Get what?" she asked.

"When you get indignant, you get a bit..." I paused, unsure if I should continue.

"A bit what?" she snapped.

"Uppity," I ventured with a cringe.

"Uppity?" she barked.

"Yeah, I thought it was an Upper East Side thing, but now I see it is a British thing. I like it," I added quickly.

"Oh," she said, placated. "Yes, well I spent more time there than I did in New York."

She sounded so sad, I wanted to ask her about it, but she changed the subject.

"I miss being in your bed," she said. "Mine is boring."

"So is mine without you in it," I retorted, and she sighed.

"Tomorrow is going to be difficult," she said quietly.

"I know." Truth was, I was dreading the meeting tomorrow. There was no getting out of it for either of us, so we would have to stick to our limited eye contact and cursory nod and try not to go all gooey around each other.

"I will have to concentrate really hard not to picture that rock-hard body of yours under your three-piece suit," she said wickedly, making my cock jump to attention.

"What about me?" I complained. "How am I supposed to look at you seriously when all I will be able to picture are those daisy chains of yours?"

She laughed and said, "Hang on a minute."

I heard her shuffling about and then my message notification dinged. I frowned at it as it jumped onto the screen and I moaned out loud. "Jesus, woman, you are evil," I stated as I stared at the image she had just sent of the very daisy chains we were just speaking of.

"Tit for tat," she said.

"What?" I asked.

"Tit for tat," she said again. "I've sent you a photo of my tits, you have to send me photo of your..."

"Oh no!" I interrupted her, horrified. I had never taken a photo of my dick and sent it someone and I wasn't about to start now.

"No fair," she pouted.

"Hey, you offered that up. I didn't agree to anything," I said, confident I had gotten out of it.

"If you think that's a good enough excuse, think again," she said in that tone that made me feel like a naughty schoolboy. "A photo! Now!" she demanded, and I gulped.

I closed my eyes and snapped away, hoping it looked alright. I quickly pressed send before I changed my mind.

"Mmmmm," she purred after a moment.

"Do not show that to anyone or else," I warned.

"Oh, you have nothing to worry about. That is for my

eyes only," she murmured. "And my hands, and my lips, and my..."

"Stop!" I yelled at her. "Do not finish that sentence or I am going to make a fool of myself."

She giggled. "Fool away," she whispered.

"No," I said firmly. I wasn't engaging in phone sex with her even if someone held a gun to my head. I had never been able to talk dirty and I would come off looking like a hopeless idiot. I started to realize that she was perhaps light-years away from me when it came to sexual inhibitions, or lack thereof. I swallowed uncomfortably and once again felt like such a prude. Was I the only person in New York who didn't engage in this type of behavior? Seems that everyone I knew was at it in some form or another.

"Don't be embarrassed, Alex," she chided him. "I am willing to bet that listening to you pleasing yourself will please me immensely."

I blushed over my entire body and stammered an unintelligible response.

Cassie took pity on me and said, "All in good time, my dear."

I snorted in response but was relieved to be off the hook.

"I will leave you to your dreams now," she said. "Goodnight, Alex."

"Goodnight, Cassie," I said. "Sweet dreams, Princess."

~Cassie~

THE MEETING HAD GONE TERRIBLY for both of us. Neither one could concentrate on a word anyone was saying and I was relieved when it had finally finished. I ducked out of the conference room quickly and back to the safety of my office, only to get a message from Alex when I returned.

"Can't do it," it read, "you have to come to my place for dinner tomorrow night."

I was going to reply that yes, I would, when Lachlan called me.

"Hey, Sweetcheeks," he said. "How's things?"

"Good," I replied. "Haven't seen you around much lately."

"I know," he said. "But I know that Rex is still out of town and I am free tomorrow night. How about wine and Chinese at your place?"

How did he know that Rex was out of town? "Yeah, sure. Sounds good." I would have to put Alex off, but it was a good distraction seeing as we weren't supposed to see each other during the week.

"Excellent," Lachlan exclaimed. "I'll be around about seven."

"See you then," I said and hung up.

I was about to reply to Alex when he sent another message to me: "Just got the all clear," followed by a happy face. I smiled and really wished I hadn't made plans with Lachlan now, but I would stick to them. I messaged back that I had plans with Lachlan but would see him on Wednesday at seven, and that I was so glad because I wanted to feel ALL of him next time. He replied with an unoriginal "same here" and I sighed. He really wasn't into being all that adventurous. I had come to realize that he was quite innocent compared to me, well maybe innocent is the wrong word...*inhibited* was more like it. It was something that I would have to fix and soon. It wasn't like the sex was boring with him, quite the opposite. This weekend had been mind-blowingly exciting, but as much as I loved sex with him the way he liked it, I needed him to like it the way I did too.

All in good time, I thought again.

TWENTY-THREE

~Cassie~

Lachlan arrived right on time on Tuesday night, barging into the apartment as if he owned the place. It was so his style. He never made a meek entrance.

"Hey, Sweetcheeks," he said, bending down from his much taller height to kiss me on the forehead.

"Hey, Lach. It's been way too long. Where've you been?" I retorted.

"Busy, busy," he said haughtily. "Sex clubs don't run themselves."

"No, I don't suppose they do," I murmured, casting a lingering glance down his body as he took his black leather jacket off. He was wearing a tight black shirt that clung to his muscular frame, showing off his sexiness. His black jeans were expensive, and he looked incredibly hot.

His mischievous brown eyes took me in, wearing sweats and a vest. "Well, at least it shows off your amazing rack," he commented, his gaze sweeping over my breasts with more interest than I had seen from him.

I didn't hate it.

"Sit," I said, scooping up my glass of red wine and curled up in the corner of the sofa. He plonked down next to me and took my feet in his lap. He started to rub them in silence, and I sighed in contentment. My bliss was suddenly halted when he dropped my feet and stood up. He started to pace, but then turned and sat directly in front of me on the coffee table.

"Lachlan? What is it?" I asked, knowing something was amiss, but also to move whatever it was along. He was freaking me out. Lach didn't do serious. He was the easy-going type.

"How's Rex?" he asked, ignoring my question.

"I don't know. I haven't spoken to him." I frowned at that. He should have returned from his business trip ages ago. I had been so wrapped up in Alex, that I hadn't even noticed that he hadn't called to say he was back.

"Hmm," Lachlan murmured. "He's still away," he added, to my surprise.

"Figured," I murmured back not wanting him to know I had no clue what was going on. "How do *you* know?" I asked, suspiciously.

Lachlan just shrugged, and then stood up again and paced away. "Look, Cassie. I am going to get right down to it." He spun around to face me again. "I am in love with you. I have always been in love with you. I know we landed in the friend zone, like, straight away. You never saw me as anything more, but I have craved you for years. I'm telling you this, finally, because I am ready to do something about it."

"What?" I stammered, also standing up to face him. "What are you saying?" My heart is thundering in my chest.

He gave me a withering glare that only he could get

away with. "I love you, Cassandra Bellingham. I want to be with you, but that isn't even the half of it."

I just blinked at him. I had no idea what to say. My mind was racing. "It isn't?" I bleated after a long pause.

"No," he stated. "As you know, I don't care about gender. Male, female, who cares. If I care about someone, I care. And I care about Rex. I fucking think he is the hottest man to have ever lived. Apart from me, of course," he laughed, smoothing down his shirt. I followed his hands and it did stir something in me. Something that, perhaps, I had pushed down assuming we were only ever "just friends". He continued, "But I also care about him. He is so fragile. It brings out the mother-hen in me. I want to look after him. But he only has eyes for you. For now." He blinked at me a couple of times, trying to gauge my reaction.

"What are you suggesting?" I asked, carefully. I thought I knew, but I needed to hear it. Have it said out loud so that my brain could process it.

He took in a deep breath. "I am suggesting that we enter into a relationship. The three of us. He will go for it if you tell him it's what you want."

I was stunned into silence. What did I say to that? I didn't even know if I wanted Lachlan that way, I also didn't know if Rex was ever going to come back after he'd run away, and I was with Alex now. Fuck! This couldn't have come at a worse time.

"I'm with someone," I blurted out, eventually.

His shrewd gaze bored into me. It was verging on uncomfortable. "Oh?" he asked.

I nodded, but before I could say anything else, he swooped in, grabbing my upper arms. "Who is he? How long? Does Rex know? Is it serious? Where did you meet him?"

I grunted and pulled my arms out of his grip. He threw me an apologetic smile. "His name is Alex, it's new, no he doesn't, it might be one day, and I met him at work," I said.

Lachlan withdrew his looming presence from me, and I breathed out, trying to take all of this in.

"Work?" Lachlan barked at me after a minute. "Oh, Cassie," he drawled, shaking his head.

"Yes, I know," I muttered.

He took in a deep breath again, his eyes closed. Then he opened them and shrugged so nonchalantly, I thought he might tell me to forget everything he had just said and stalk off.

When he opened his eyes again, they were steady as they found mine. I stared at him, waiting for what he had to say. "So, we have a fourth," he says. "I don't care. If you like him, he isn't a dick, so all good."

"What?" I said again for what seemed like the millionth time. "You are still suggesting we pursue a...a...four-way relationship?" My voice was a high-pitched squeak. I couldn't fathom it. How would it work?

Lachlan snorted as he somehow read my mind. "You have three holes, Cas. You figure it out."

"Fuck! Lach!" I yelled at him, scandalized. It was like that woman at the sex ball. But then I remembered that I had wondered what it would be like.

"He wouldn't go for it," I said with conviction.

"Who, Rex or this Alex guy?"

"Alex. Rex...both. I don't know," I wailed. "Why are you doing this to me?"

"Because I love you and I want him. If you two are already together then I get everything I want. Don't tell me you haven't thought about me that way?" he said it lightly, but his eyes betrayed the seriousness behind it. He waited.

"Of course I have," I said softly. "At the beginning, but you never made a move, so I thought you just wanted to be friends, and I was okay with that."

"I am not okay with that. Not anymore. I want you, Cassie, I do. I am putting it out there now. Talk to Rex, if you asked him, he would do it. I know it. He loves you too," he said softly.

How would I even broach this subject with him? I had no idea. And what about Alex? Christ. There is no way he would accept this if he didn't even want to send me a dick-pic. But I couldn't deny that the mere thought of having them all to myself was a very appealing one. My imagination ran wild with all of the possibilities now that I was getting used to the idea of it. I realized in that moment that I wanted it. I just didn't know if I could *have* it.

"Rex doesn't swing both ways," I blurted out suddenly.

Lachlan gave me an arrogant smile. "You leave that to me, baby. You just need to talk to him. Tell him this is what you want."

"And if he refuses and I lose him?" I challenged him, forgetting about the fact that I might have already anyway.

"Then I will be here to pick up the pieces. I am done waiting around, Cassie. Speak to your men, and you know where to find me."

And with that said, he barged back out of the apartment in the same manner he had entered, leaving me reeling with everything that he'd said.

"Fuck!" I shouted at the elevator doors just to make myself feel better. "Fuck," I repeated more quietly.

I sank down onto the sofa and grabbed my abandoned wine and drank the entire glass back in one gulp.

THE LANDLINE RANG and I froze. The same distorted voice came through with the same message telling me that I was playing with fire. I'd had enough of this guy. I yanked the phone out of the wall and wrapped the cord around it tightly. I shoved it into the trash and grabbed the trash bag in my fist. I stormed out of the front doors and chucked it with great gusto down the chute. I heard it clunking as it made its way down. I dusted my hands off and went back inside, feeling marginally better about that, but still all over the place about Lachlan and his proposal. Did I want this? Yes, now that it was sinking in, I did want it. Did I want three men in my bed all night, every night? Uhm, yes. We'd cuddle some nights. It's not like we had to have sex all of the time. Or would we? Who knows? Did I love Lachlan in the way he wanted me to? No, but I *did* love him and weren't the best relationships developed from friendships? Did I find him all kinds of hot? Hell yes. He was divine. Now that I allowed myself to think about him that way, I almost started to drool. How could I not have thought about it before? Would Rex go for it? I had no idea. No idea if he would even call me when he got back into town. Would Alex go for it? Hell no. There isn't even a chance that he would. I sighed. I, once again, had some thinking to do. But nothing could be decided until Rex returned. I slunk off to bed, suddenly exhausted.

———

THE NEXT EVENING, I was sitting at the kitchen counter going over a few notes from work. I was due to leave for Alex's in about half an hour and I wanted to get this done. I knew I was letting my professional side down with my personal life getting in the way. I had to decide what do and fucking soon. I growled in annoyance, but my phone buzzing next to me interrupted my thoughts. I frowned at it, set to ignore it, but it was my grandmother. I picked it up quickly.

"Grandma, is everything okay?" I asked in a mild panic.

I heard my grandmother sniffle slightly and my stomach dropped about a mile. "Yes, dear. Your grandfather and I are fine, but I do have some bad news, dear."

I gulped. "What is it? Mother?"

"No, no, your mother is fine. It is Richard, dear. There has been a terrible accident," Grandma said.

It took me a moment to remember who Richard was. "Why? What's happened?" I asked, relieved that at least it wasn't a member of my family. I disliked my parents, but I didn't want any harm to come to them.

Grandma sniffed again and a dread started to well up in me. "He's been shot, Cassie. He's dead."

"What?" I asked, the blood draining from my face. "How? When? What happened?"

"In London. He was opening a new center for his foundation and he was shot dead right there in broad daylight!" My grandmother's voice went up a few octaves.

"Oh my God," I breathed. "Was it an accident, or was he..." I didn't know what to call it...murdered?

"The police say it was a long-distance shot, but the precision of it means it was likely intended for him." Grandma started to cry outright now, and my heart ached. She was very close with Richard's parents. That's why she had set us up on a date, hoping that we would get together.

"Oh, Grandma," I soothed. "I am so sorry. Please pass on my condolences to his parents. It is an awful thing. I don't understand it."

"I will, dear, thank you. He was such a good boy, so

generous and kind, helping those poor children get back on their feet."

I knew from their conversations that Richard ran a charitable foundation that helped rehabilitate teens and young adults whose lives had been destroyed by drug and alcohol abuse. He gave them jobs, a place to stay and counseling. I couldn't imagine for the life of me why someone would want to kill him.

"I should go, Cassie. Margaret and Richard are beside themselves. I just wanted to let you know as I know you were getting close."

Well, as a ruse. I felt dreadful that I had intended to use him to cover up my relationship with Alex. "Take care, Grandma. I'll speak to you again soon."

"Goodbye, dear," Grandma said and with a final sniff, she disconnected the call.

Holy crap. With the exception of my Aunt Rebecca, I had never known anyone personally who had died before. And, certainly, not by being shot. I was horrified and now that the information was sinking in, I thought I was going into mild shock.

My phone going off startled me back to the present. It was Rex. I took the call because I needed to know when he was returning from his trip. The sooner I spoke to him and got it over with, the better.

"Hi," I said.

"Hi, Cassandra. Are you well?" he asked quietly.

"Yes, fine," I replied. "Well, in a bit of shock I suppose." I told him of my grandmother's phone call.

"Oh," he said as I finished up. He cleared his throat. "You were close with him?"

"Well, no, not really. His parents are friends of the

family. It is just... I don't know why someone would do that?"

He was silent.

"Sorry," I said. "I know I am being all maudlin. When will you be back?"

"I will be back Saturday," he said. "Sorry, that I haven't contacted you before. It's been...busy and I got delayed. Can I see you?"

"Yes," I said immediately. "Come to the penthouse as soon as you get back. I need to see you."

"I will see you then," he said. "Is everything all right, apart from your friend? You sound tired."

"Oh, it's nothing," I said, glancing at where the phone used to be.

"Cassandra, what it is? You can tell me," he said, getting worried.

I debated for a moment whether to tell him about the creepy phone calls and then, resigned, I said, "It's just these crank phone calls I've been getting. It's unnerving and especially so now."

"Crank phone calls?" he asked sharply. "When did they start? What do they say?"

I filled him in.

"Have you told the police?" he asked.

"Oh no, no," I said feeling foolish now. "Like I said, it's nothing."

"I have a friend who can trace the calls. Leave it with me. Once we have a location, you can go to the police, okay?"

~Rex~

I HATED that I wasn't there to protect her, instead I was on a ferry crossing the English Channel.

"No, Rex, it's not necessary," Cassie insisted, but I was having none of it and she eventually relented and gave me her landline number. I already knew it but went through the pretense of writing it down anyway. I was going to find out who was calling my angel and when I was through with them, they wouldn't be able to speak, never mind use a phone ever again. I was also going to make sure she was guarded until I could get back to her. I replaced my cell phone in my backpack and pulled out the burner cell. I went out on deck and dialed the Captain. I told him briefly of my conversation and gave him Cassandra's number, not giving him a name. Then I hung up and rang the security firm that I knew the Captain used, giving them Cassandra's details and to maintain covert cover until I returned. Then I threw the phone over the railing and I watched it bob and then sink under the waves.

I decided in that moment that this was my final job. I was done. I had neither thought about, nor cared about, the family and friends my targets left behind. It was different when one of those people was Cassandra. She had sounded so upset, but I had nothing to say to her. I mean, what was I supposed to say? Sorry, Cassandra, it was me who killed your friend, but I have no idea why and for whom? No, it ended there. I just didn't want to do it anymore.

TWENTY-FOUR

~Cassie~

The phone rang again. I was getting a bit tired of this now. "Uncle Teddy?" I said in mock disbelief. "This is a surprise."

"I know, girl. I have been very remiss in keeping in contact," he said and chuckled. "Are you keeping well?"

"Yes, yes I am fine. Busy, but that's the job," I said brightly.

"And how is Bellingham Corp treating you? I was surprised the old man relinquished control, thought he'd hang on to the bitter end," Teddy said with a loud guffaw.

I returned the laugh and said, "You and me both. I think Grandma Ruby had enough. Put her foot down."

"I always liked the old broad," he said. "The only one that could make him do anything."

"Very true," I agreed. "So, to what do I owe the pleasure? You heard from Dad?"

"Just thought I would check in. Make sure everything was going well? And no, sorry to say that I haven't, but that isn't unusual for Damien. He is a world-class ass."

"No kidding," I said wryly. "But yeah, everything is good. Are you in New York?"

"I am, we should do dinner," Teddy said.

"Absolutely. I'll get Marjorie to set it up," I said.

"Ah, you've only been in the job a few weeks and you already get your people to set a date with me," he said, teasing me.

I snorted and said, "Like you could tell me if you were free tomorrow night without consulting with Stacey."

"Well, you have me there," he admitted grudgingly. "You sure everything is fine with you?"

"Of course," I said. "All good."

"Good," he said.

"I will speak to you soon," I said, and we said our goodbyes.

I replaced the phone on the counter with a smile. I missed my uncle. He and Aunt Rebecca had been better parents to me than my real parents when I was much younger. They had lived in London for a while when I was at boarding school, so for a year I had someplace to go during the holidays. Everything had changed though when Aunt Rebecca had died. She had been killed seven years ago by a drunk driver. Uncle Teddy had been devastated and he had closed himself off from everybody, until exactly one year later he came out of his shell like nothing had ever happened and went on to live the high life. It was strange, but I supposed people grieved in different ways.

I huffed in annoyance as my phone rang yet again and I answered it.

"Hi," I said.

"Hey, are you on your way?" Alex asked.

I quickly flicked up my wrist to look at my watch and groaned. "Oh, Alex. I'm so sorry." I was already half an hour late.

"Is everything okay?" he asked.

"Not really," I replied and told him about Richard.

"Shit," Alex said. "He's dead?"

"Yeah," I said and sighed. "I'm sorry, babe. I am just not up for coming over tonight. I think I'm just going to go to bed. Is that okay?"

"Uh, yeah I guess so," he said.

"I'm sorry. I hope you didn't go to too much trouble?" I asked.

"No, no trouble."

I smiled. "I will make it up to you, I promise."

"Mm, I will hold you to that. Go and get some rest, Princess. I'll speak to you tomorrow," he said.

"Bye, baby," I murmured and disconnected, relieved that I had another night to think about Lachlan and his tempting arrangement.

~Alex~

I LOOKED across at the candlelit dinner I had just spent the last hour making. I wasn't all that hungry now. I blew out the candles and packed the dinner away. I thought back to what Cassie had told me about Richard. I had Googled the guy after Cassie said she was going to see him again in order to keep up pretenses, and he had come up with the whole "good guy" spiel. But I wasn't convinced. No one was that squeaky clean, so I dug a little deeper, being a bit of a computer nerd, it wasn't that difficult for me. It took some finding, but I had happened upon the skeleton in the Pomfries IV's closet. Turned out, in college he had been a bit of a party boy. Nothing too crazy, until he wrapped his car around a tree and killed a girl while driving under the influence, of not only a boatload of alcohol, but drugs as well. The girl's parents had called for a lynch mob, but Pomfries's pockets ran deep. It had never reached court and was nicely buried. I wondered if that had something to do with not only his choice in charities, but why he had been killed as well. Still, I felt sorry for the guy. No one deserved that kind of ending, but I had to admit in a small, dark place that I was relieved that Cassie didn't have to see him again. I had been reluctant to dredge up that guy's past with her as it would make me look all stalkery and possessive. I didn't want her to think I was "that guy." I thought perhaps I was "that guy," though, with her. She had bewitched me, and I was falling hard and fast. I wanted nothing more than to be with her every moment of every day. I checked my phone again for the email I was waiting for and still nothing.

I was restless, so I pulled on my running gear and took a swift jog around the neighborhood before showering and crashing.

IT WAS Friday before we managed to get together again for our date. Cassie invited me over to *her* apartment that time. I was excited to see her place. Now I could properly picture her here in my dreams.

"Fantastic," I said with a smile, as I looked around at the

grandeur of the place. It drove home the fact that she was so out of my league, I was lucky she even gave me the time of day.

"It's okay," she said modestly.

She let me have a good look around. I started to wander down the corridor where there was one door at the end. I assumed it was her bedroom so with a sassy look back I twisted the handle.

It was locked.

Cassie leapt forward and steered me in the other direction.

"Wrong way," she muttered, taking my hand. She led me in the opposite direction to her bedroom and I laughed.

"What, no dinner first?" I asked, even though I was prepared and had already eaten. "So demanding."

"I have been waiting all week for you, dinner can wait," she said.

I needed no persuading after that. I kissed her, nipping at her full lips, my hands aching to touch her skin, when we were interrupted by a knock at the front door.

Cassie pulled away and frowned. She hesitated but then went to the front door and peeped through the hole.

She opened the door, with a smile. I stood right behind her, peering over her shoulder, intrigued as to who it was that she would let in while I was there.

"Well?" a hunky blonde guy demanded of her before she had a chance to say anything.

I narrowed my eyes at him. Who the fuck was this douche? And why was I suddenly going around thinking all the guys I met were good-looking?

"Lachlan," she said calmly. "Nice to see you too."

"Humph," he retorted. "And about that...why am I

forced to come up here like the help? Why is the elevator locked?"

I blinked down at Cassie, expecting an answer as to who this asshole was.

She was about to say something when the guy finally caught sight of me over Cassie's shoulder. There was an awkward silence as he glared at me. I stuck my hand out and said, "Hi, I'm Alex. A...friend of Cassie's."

"Lachlan," he said, taking my hand and gripping it so tightly it neatly broke. "Also, a friend of Cassie's."

Lachlan released my hand and gave Cassie a raised eyebrow. "I see," he said, his attitude adjusting to one doused with charm. "Alex. I have heard about you."

"Lach," Cassie said, almost warning him. She put a hand to his chest to stop him from coming further into the apartment. "We are on a date, if you don't mind?"

"Oh really?" he asked, his eyes still on me. "Gotten to the good part yet?" he added with a smirk, finally turning to look back at Cassie. I breathed out in relief. I had felt like he was checking me out, or something.

"No, you interrupted," she said tightly. "Can I call you later?"

"Sure," he said. "But when you make that call, I expect an answer one way or the other." He gave her a meaningful look that excluded me completely and it made me nervous. Then his eyes snapped back to mine and he gave me a raking once-over that made my skin prickle.

"I can see why you caught Cassie's attention," he said. "You are a complete smoke-show."

Cassie snorted into her hand. She clearly found that amusing. I, however, did not. I was not used to having guys make note of my looks. Although, I had done the same to him, I at least, had kept it to myself.

Lachlan looked back at Cassie and nodded. "I approve," he said and then kissed her forehead and left abruptly.

"Care to share?" I asked as she shut the door.

"Not yet. I will, but first, I would rather you..."

I didn't hear what she said after that because she stripped off her top and bra and all I could focus on were those daisy chains.

I PULLED HER TO ME, and she clung to me as we kissed. I picked her up and carried her to her bed, placing her down gently.

She ripped the rest of her clothes off before she started on mine.

"I'm not waiting anymore; I want to feel every last inch of you inside me."

Her words drove me crazy; she always knew exactly what to say to me to get me all riled up.

"Oh, Cassie," I said as her hands undid my pants and she pulled out my rock-hard cock. She ran her fingers lightly over it, making me twitch. I couldn't wait, I didn't *want* to wait. I wanted to be inside her and finally feel her hot wetness against my skin now, and nothing, not even taking my pants off properly, was going to stop me. I pushed her back and rammed into her as she cried out.

"Oh, God yes," she screamed as I pounded into her again and again until she was rippling around me in ecstasy.

"Cassie," I groaned as I let go, thrusting deep inside her. "God, you feel so good."

"Cassandra?" I heard a distraught voice say her name.

She looked at me. I looked back at her, and then we both turned to the door.

"Fuck," I said, jumping up and pulling my pants up. "What the fuck?" I yanked Cassie behind me protectively as she said, "Rex! What are you doing here? How did you get in?"

Rex was glowering at us, looking ready to kill.

"Rex?" Cassie said again, gently pushing me to the side.

"You said to come over when I got back, and it's Friday," he said shortly. "It's our day."

I looked from Cassie to Rex and my stomach dropped to my feet.

"You said you would be back tomorrow," Cassie said desperately. She looked at me in panic and then flinched from the anger that she must have seen on my face.

"So, you just replaced me while I was gone?" Rex asked bitterly and turned away from us.

He looked like his heart was breaking and it made me even more angry.

"Wait," Cassie said, rapidly throwing her clothes back on. I was still staring at her as I jerked my own shirt back on.

I was heartbroken, but above all, I was disgusted as the pieces fell into place. "You're the angel?" I spat at her as I marched into the sitting room behind Rex, who had disappeared that way. "*She's* the angel?" I asked again to Rex. He stayed stonily silent. I put my hand on the back of my neck, tapping fiercely as I muttered, "Of course she is."

"Alex, wait," Cassie said. "I can explain."

"Oh, no need," I said, holding my hands up. "I have quite the vivid picture of the two of you together." I forced the bile back down as I remembered the bite marks and scratches and worst of all, the big, black bruises, that she had inflicted on him. An image of the bruises around Rex's wrists flashed through my head, along with the faint yellow marking I remembered seeing on Cassie's wrist the Sunday she came to tell me she wanted us to be together. I nearly threw up as I realized she had been with Rex the night she left the ball. The night before she came to me.

"Alex," she said softly. "Please just listen to me," she begged.

"No," I said, shaking my head. "What you and he do together...it's *sick*. I can't believe you would do that."

The shock on Cassie's face tore at me. I knew my words had been harsh, but this wasn't anywhere near anything I could accept. I might have listened had it just been about sex, but all the rest? No, I was so out of there. She might have been an angel, but she had just fallen from grace and I had to get away from her, from both of them.

I shot a look of hatred at Rex, who just stood there like someone had punched him in the gut. I thought about doing it for a minute, but the guy could probably flatten me with little to no effort, and besides, I didn't want to waste another second around the two of them. With another look of revulsion, mixed with sorrow, at Cassie, I stalked out of the apartment, slamming the door closed behind me.

Cassie was hot on my heels as I stabbed the button for the main elevator.

"Alex, please," Cassie said frantically. "It's not what you think. Just listen to me, please." She grabbed my arm, but I shook her off roughly.

"Don't touch me," I snarled at her and she drew her hands back swiftly.

"Alex," she whimpered as the tears fell down her face. I stepped into the elevator and without even looking at her, I let the doors slide shut.

~Cassie~

"ALEX," I screamed as I beat my fists against the elevator door. My sorrow tore through me. I had no idea why he had gone so hostile. I could understand that he was mad because he thought I was sleeping with Rex, but he hadn't even let me explain. The look of disgust on his face had completely thrown me. I had to get to him, to speak to him and make him understand my relationship with Rex. I marched back into my apartment and came to a halt as Rex was still standing there. I had forgotten all about him as Alex had made his getaway. *Just one more person to abandon me.*

I just stared at Rex who was staring back at me. It didn't escape my notice that he *hadn't* abandoned me. At least not this time.

"How long?" Rex asked.

"A week," I said. "This is why I wanted to talk to you, Rex. It is getting complicated and I have a proposition for you, but now isn't the time." I kept seeing the look on Alex's face and it made me sick.

"A week?" he scoffed, ignoring the rest of what I'd said.

"We've been together, properly, a week. It's been going on longer than that." I felt the need to defend myself.

"You mean you've been screwing him for a week, while I have been away," Rex said bitterly. "I wanted more from you, Cassandra. I thought you wanted the same?" He said it so sadly my heart would have broken for him had it not already been breaking for myself.

I *had* wanted more, but he had run away from me. Just like Alex had. Just like everyone had in my life. I was all alone, again, and the tears started to fall. I wanted to say more to Rex, but I couldn't find the words. He turned from me and left me, crying and alone in my apartment, with no idea how this perfectly wonderful night had gone so terribly wrong.

TWENTY-FIVE

~Alex~

I ran.

I ran out of the building, down the street, past the bus stop, past the subway. I just wanted to run as far away from her as I could get. My imagination kept going to what she and Rex were doing right now. They were no doubt laughing at me for being so conservative, while they chained each other up and inflicted pain on each other before they fucked until dawn.

The pain in my heart intensified and I had to stop. I bent over breathing in deeply to stop myself from vomiting.

Those images were swiftly being replaced with the ones I had buried deep, deep down. The ones that I had wanted to forget, the ones I knew had been responsible for shaping my conventional sexual outlook. I didn't want to see it, I didn't want to relive it, but it wormed its way into my mind and then it was all I could see.

The kid, about sixteen or so, naked and tied to a chair in my mother's basement. I remembered the look of fear on his face. I would never forget it, as hard as I tried. I saw my mother, trussed up in a slutty leather outfit that made her look ridiculous and old. I heard her wicked laugh as she flicked her wrist back and the whip cracked through the air before it landed on the boy's chest with a sickening noise. She whipped the kid again and again as he whimpered and I watched in horror, unable to move. The bald guy in the corner was laughing and encouraging my mother to hit the kid harder. I knew I had to do something. I wasn't a big guy. I was scrawny and fairly geeky. I had been called a nerd all through school, but I couldn't just stand there and let this happen. My mother tossed down the whip, stripped off her clothes, and straddled the kid, who looked like he was about to throw up. That's when I jumped forward. I grabbed my mother by her hair and pulled her off him. I might have been skinny, but I was sure I could handle my mother. I yelled at her for being a filthy whore and, running on pure instinct and rage, I had slapped her across the face. She had fallen to her knees, while the bald guy just kept on laughing like this was all a game to him. I had turned to the teenager in the chair and started to untie him. That's when the bald guy stopped laughing. The basement became as silent as a mausoleum as he strode forward and twisted my arm tightly enough to snap my wrist. I howled in pain, but I wasn't giving up. I struggled and fought and got the kid free enough so that he could get away.

"Run," I'd shouted to the terrified teenager who was staring at me like a deer in headlights.

"Get out," I shouted again, before I was punched in the face and with a sickening crunch, my glasses broke, and so did my nose.

"Mind your own business, kid," the bald guy had snarled at me. I'd dropped like a stone, no match for this guy, and I got a swift kick to the ribs. "Get back here, Evan!" the bald guy yelled. The kid bolted like a jackrabbit and as naked as a jaybird. He launched up the basement stairs after him as I staggered to my feet. My mother was cowering in the corner, crying and scared. I had never been fond of her, but in that moment, I hated her. She was disgusting, a repulsive abusive monster that I never wanted to see again. I made it to the bottom of the stairs when Baldy came back. "He got away," he said as he thumped down the stairs in his heavy boots. "You are going to have to pay for that, kid," he added as he advanced on me.

I had been hospitalized after that attack. My sister had found me and made sure I got there. I was in a coma for a week and when I came out of it, I was alone. My mother, scared of suffering the same fate at the hands of the bald guy, had scampered and taken my sister with her. True to my word, that was the last time I saw her. She had tried to reach out to me, but I wasn't interested. I would never be interested in seeing her face again.

When I left the hospital a few weeks later, spring break was over and I went straight back to college, I made a vow that when I finally lost my virginity, it would be to a woman that I loved and treasured and I would never be like my mother. I would never treat sex as a brutal act and I would never treat someone as she had that day and above all else, I would never be that scrawny kid again. I joined the gym and made sure I was skilled enough to defend myself should the need arise, but no matter how much I worked out, I was always going to be more lean-muscular as opposed to rippling, bulging, and Rex-sized.

My stomach heaved and I leaned over and vomited

beside the building I was leaning against. The passersby gave me a wide berth, assuming I was drunk or something, but I didn't care what any of them thought in that moment.

My breathing slowed and I felt less nauseous. I put my hands up to my eyes and, even though I wore contacts now, I could still feel the glasses on my face and how it had felt when they had been smashed. I pushed off from the building and walked slowly, still unable to get my head around the fact that the woman I'd thought I was falling in love with, was just like the woman I hated more than anything.

~Rex~

I LEFT Cassandra's on foot. I had driven my car there, but I left it in the parking garage. I wanted to walk to clear my head and my rage. All I kept seeing and hearing was my beautiful angel and that Alex fucker, going at it like their lives depended on it. It made me sick, and angry, but most of all sad because they had been in her bed. That immaculate, white bed that I had so badly wanted to be in with her but was too afraid. I didn't know what was going to happen next. I had walked out on her again because to stay would have been my undoing. I was unraveling fast and if I didn't find a way to fix it, the destruction I would cause would be catastrophic. I walked and seethed and thought of every way that I could make Alex pay for being with my Cassandra.

I eventually found myself in a familiar neighborhood, in

a familiar apartment building, outside a familiar door. I had no idea how I had gotten there, but I didn't care. I must have ended up there for a reason. I knocked and waited and when the door opened, I pushed my way in and closed it with a bang.

~Cassie~

I WAS DISTRAUGHT. First Alex had walked out on me and then Rex. Why did this keep happening to me? I was far from a whiny brat and long ago gave up feeling sorry for myself, but I just had to ask, was I so unlovable that every person I came into contact with just couldn't stand to be around me? I paced, grabbed a bottle of wine and poured out a glass as I called Alex for the hundredth time. It didn't even ring anymore, it was just going straight to voicemail. I picked up the glass, then put it back down and picked up the bottle instead. I took a big swig and choked back a sob. I tried to call Rex, but his phone was switched off and even Lachlan was unavailable. I sank further into my despair and I realized I wasn't surprised to find I was all alone. This was how it usually ended for me. I had hoped it would be different with Alex, even with the obstacles in our way, I had thought he was a decent guy. A guy who would at least give me a chance to explain, but he was just like all the others. This was a far cry from the arrangement that Lachlan had described to me. In that arrangement I would never be alone again. I wanted it. I needed it. I was going to make it happen come hell or high water. I finished off the bottle of wine and passed out on the sofa, clutching my phone in case Alex called me back.

UNSURPRISINGLY, there were no missed calls or messages when I woke up with the hangover from the abyss on Saturday. I showered and jumped a mile when the phone rang. I leapt on it, but it was only my grandfather. I wanted to ignore it in case Alex called, but reluctantly answered and then wished I hadn't.

"Girl," my grandfather barked at me. "You have some explaining to do." I could hear him pacing and in spite of his tone, smiled as I pictured him.

"Hello to you too, Granddaddy. What is the problem?" I asked, in the dark about his mood.

"This!" he declared, and I could hear him prodding something.

"Sorry, you are going to have to be more specific. *You* may be all-seeing but the rest of us mere mortals need details," I said dryly, and he snorted down the phone.

"I will send it to you," he said shortly.

I waited while he emailed whatever it was to me. My grandfather may have seen eighty a good few years ago, but he was just as savvy when it came to technology as I was. I peered at my iPad as it came through and my face blanched. It was a photo of me and Alex at the ball on the dance floor. We were cozied up to each other and smiling. I knew we had been flirting madly when he had asked me to be with him.

"Isn't that your new V.P. that you seem to be getting cozy with?" he snapped.

"Yes, it is. But it's not what you think, we were just

dancing." I had to defend myself, my grandfather would hit the roof if he found out about our relationship. *What relationship?* I pushed that aside to deal with momentarily.

"Looks like more than just dancing. I warned you, Cassandra, I will not tolerate this kind of behavior," he said in that tone that didn't leave room for an argument.

I sighed. I wondered where on Earth he had gotten the photo from in the first place. I had never seen it before, so it hadn't been one of the official ones that had been taken. "Granddaddy," I said in a placating tone, "I can assure you; it is strictly professional."

He harrumphed at me down the phone and I knew he was accepting my story. Just barely. "Make sure you keep it that way, girl."

"Promise, promise," I said as I crossed my fingers. I was so going to hell.

"Very well. Anything else you need to discuss with me?" he asked.

I smiled at his choice of words. "No, everything is just fine," I lied. Things couldn't be more *wrong* if I'd tried.

"Good," he said, all genial again. "Must go, your mother is waiting for us."

I felt like I had been slapped. I sat heavily on the kitchen stool.

"Cassie, dear?" I heard my grandmother's voice come over the line as I heard grandfather muttering something in the background. "Cassie? Are you still there?"

"Yes, Grandma," I said. "You're seeing them?"

She sighed and said, "Yes, dear. We had no idea they were in Cannes when we arrived. Suzanne invited us to their yacht for dinner. We..."

"Of course," I said stiffly. "Of course, you have to go."

There was an awkward silence. "I'll give them your love, shall I?" Grandma ventured.

I shook my head vehemently. "No, that's fine. Don't mention you spoke to me."

"Cassie," she started.

"Just leave it, okay?" I said. I was not in the mood for this right now and I wanted to get off the phone.

"Okay, dear," Grandma said. "I had better go, your grandfather is getting restless. He has these harebrained schemes, but I don't think he thinks it all the way through. He likes the idea of sailing around the world but doesn't realize that once you get into open water, there's no getting off the damned thing." She sighed a long-suffering sigh, which made me snicker in spite of my dreadful mood. Sounded exactly like my grandfather.

"Okay, Grandma. Take care. I'll speak to you soon."

"Bye, dear."

I placed my phone on the counter and felt even more alone than I had before.

TWENTY-SIX

~Rex~

I made a quiet, hasty exit. I had woken up and not even realized where I was or what I had done. I wanted to go back to Cassandra and beg her forgiveness, beg her to take me back, for real this time. But I had seen how upset she was over that Alex guy. Now was not the time to turn up and confuse her. She would make a rushed decision and probably regret it later. It killed me to stay away, but I did.

Lachlan had advised me this was the best course of action, and I believed him. He told me that Cassandra cared about me and that I needed to give her a chance to explain. Even if he hadn't told me all of that, I would've gone to her anyway. I didn't care about her indiscretion. She had her reasons and I was willing to listen. Last night I was upset and confused, but I saw everything clearly now. I wanted to be with her. It was as simple as that.

I went home, sat, waited and watched the clock go

around and around. Eventually, I went to the laptop and looked up Alex's address. I hacked into the gym records and found him easily. Alex Monaghan, lived in Greenwich Village. That was so close to here, I could go and...what exactly? Cassandra would hate me if I hurt the guy. So again, I did nothing and sat and waited. There was one situation I could deal with, though, and I picked up my new burner cell. I dialed the Captain and resigned my post, much to the Captain's disappointment. I breathed a sigh of relief and felt like a small piece of the heavy weight that was on my shoulders lifted. I could start making amends. I could start to work towards being good enough for the woman that I loved.

TWENTY-SEVEN

~Lachlan~

I had watched Rex silently leave that morning. I had pretended to be asleep so that I could watch him through narrowed eyes. He had spent the night on, not in, the bed with me, tossing and turning. The man had no clue how to sleep properly. I am glad that he came to me after this disaster. I'd hoped that Cassie would speak to him before he found out about that Alex guy. But I had managed to talk him around. He'd been dangerous when he arrived here last night. I knew he was ready to do something really stupid, but when I told him that Cassie cared about him, he crumpled like a paper doll. It hadn't taken much convincing after that to get him to listen to me about giving her another chance.

I knew he would. He would go to her tomorrow and she would tell him what she wanted. I didn't need to ask her to know what that was. She wanted all of us. It was obvious.

And if none of us made her choose, then why should she? She could *have* us all.

I poured myself a drink and settled down to read as a distraction from my racing thoughts. I couldn't wait for tomorrow. I was going to give Cassie enough time to speak to Rex and then I was going up there to take what I wanted. Finally. It had been a long time coming and I was anxious to have the woman that I loved tell me that she wanted me.

~Alex~

I HAD KEPT my phone switched off all weekend. I didn't want to speak to anyone, especially Cassie. I was trying to work through my hurt and anger and hearing her voice would only make it worse.

I turned it back on Monday morning on the way to work and immediately regretted it. I had about fifteen voicemails, all from Cassie, and the same in text messages, begging me to hear her out. That she needed to explain to me about Rex and that she wanted to be with me. But nothing, whatsoever, about the thing that was really eating me up inside. She had no idea how I felt about it. I wanted to tell her, explain to her why I couldn't be with her, but I couldn't put it into words. With a sigh, I switched my phone back off and disappeared into the crowds heading into the building to get to work.

I MADE it through Monday without seeing her, but I wasn't so lucky on Tuesday. We passed in the lobby. I saw her before she saw me, and our encounter was unavoidable. My heart jackhammered in my chest as she came towards me, engrossed in whatever her companion had to say. She finally saw me, but I had no idea what to say to her or how to act. I fixed my eyes straightforward and completely blanked her. I felt her eyes on me as I strode away and I regretted being so cold with her, but I was still so disgusted with her behavior it was all I could do at that moment in time.

~Cassie~

I WATCHED Alex walk past me without even a glance in my direction. I was devastated, but then I found my anger. How dare he? How dare he treat me so callously? I had tried my best to tell him over voicemail and text message that I needed to speak to him to explain, and yet he acted like he didn't even know me. I dismissed my colleague, who was trying to go over the notes of my latest meeting with me, but I wasn't interested. All I wanted to do was head home.

I GOT a surprise when I stepped off the elevator into the penthouse.

"Hi," I said warily to Rex who was standing staring out

of the window. I carefully put my briefcase down and waited.

"Hi," he said, turning around. "Sorry, I let myself in. Habit." He shrugged so I did too.

"I'm sorry about the way I acted the other night. I was a complete asshole. I should never have left you like that," he said. "Especially as you were so upset."

I blinked at him. I hadn't expected that. "Yeah, you were," I said to his amusement, glad that I could tell him that without it coming directly from me.

He indicated the sofa and I sat down next to him.

"I know," he said. "I was surprised and more than a little hurt to find you with someone. You had never indicated that there was someone else in your life, and to be honest, Cassandra, I thought we were..." He trailed off and looked at me, trying to gauge my reaction.

"I don't know what we were," I ventured carefully.

"But that Saturday night of the ball, you were going to make a choice, weren't you?" he pressed. "You were going to see if we could become more?"

I stood up, unsure what to say to him. This was so unexpected. I didn't think Rex would come back after he left. God knows, Alex hadn't bothered to talk to me. I had to organize my thoughts. See if he was here to come back or just to have closure. I knew that if he said he wanted to come back to me, then I would tell him about Lachlan and his proposal.

I paced and then turned back to him. "I wanted to," I said. "Alex had come to me that night to ask me to be with him, in secret. I told him I had to think about it because we work together. I knew it would be a difficult relationship, no matter how much I wanted to be with him."

I saw the pain of my words cut across Rex like a knife, but he let me continue.

"That night, I saw a different side to you," I said softly. "You were a bit more relaxed and I felt that we could try to be something more. When we got back here, I messed it up," I said woefully. "I tried to show you what I wanted, but I should have *told* you. I should have made it clear. Then you panicked and..."

Rex made a choking noise. "Panicked?" he asked wryly. "I would have picked a more manly word for it."

I giggled quietly and said, "Still, you, panicked in a manly way, and you ran from me. I thought that maybe I had read it wrong. That you didn't want me that way." I sat back down, and he took my hand. "I struggle with people running from me..."

"You didn't read it wrong. I did want you; I do want you, that way. I just...I'm not good with these things, Cassandra. I need things spelling out and I need to know that if we crossed that line again, that this time there is no going back." I saw him draw in a deep breath and hold it.

I chewed my lip. I knew Rex needed, deserved, an answer right away, but Alex and I hadn't resolved anything yet. As far as I was concerned, we were still dating and just going through a bad patch. Admittedly, it was a very bad patch, seeing as he hadn't spoken to me for days, but still.

"There's something else," I ventured cautiously. I might as well get it out there before I chickened out.

"What is it?" he asked as I paused for a lengthy time to figure out how to say it.

"Lachlan came to me the other night. He told me some things that surprised me. He told me something that he wanted and, while I was caught off guard at the time, I haven't been able to stop thinking about it since."

"What does he want?" he asked stiffly.

"Me," I said with a nervous laugh. His face went dark, but then I added, "And you," and his face went puce.

"Excuse me?" he asked, his eyes swimming with confusion.

"Exactly how it sounds," I said lightly, taking his hand. "He wants to be with us, in a relationship. He said that he loves me, always has, but that he needs to be with you too."

Rex stood up and walked away from me. He stared out of the window. Time ticked along.

Minutes passed.

I kept quiet so that he could gather his own thoughts. I didn't want to rush him into making a decision, as it would probably rush him right out of the door. I knew I wanted him to tell me yes. I would have to deal with Alex as and when he decided to speak to me. But right there, right then. I knew what I wanted.

"Is this what you want?" he asked me eventually, still staring out of the window.

I stood up and moved across to stand next to him. "Yes," I said bravely. Hoping I wasn't making a massive mistake. I could end up with nothing.

He nodded briefly and went back to being quiet. I was about to leave him to it, go and get myself a drink or something to stop the nerves from eating me alive, when he spoke again.

"He loves you?" he asked.

I nodded.

"He loves...*me*?"

I blinked. "Uhm, you'd have to ask him that. I just know that he wants you."

"I don't...I have never..." he floundered; his face stricken when he looked at me.

"It's okay," I said to him shaking my head. "I wanted to lay the cards on the table. If you don't want this..."

"No," he said quickly. "I didn't say that."

My heart jack hammered.

"I'm trying, badly, to say that I have never been with a man. I don't think I am attracted to men. I haven't ever thought I was. Does he think that I am?" he asked desperately.

"No," I said, trying not to laugh at his uncertainty. I wasn't laughing at him; it was my nerves about to get shot. If he didn't say something about what I really wanted him to and soon, I was going to die of nervousness, if that were possible. "They are his feelings. I am sure if you speak to him, you can tell him what you want."

"I want you," he said quickly as he grabbed my hands. "Do you want me?"

"Yes," I said straight away to reassure him and to move this conversation along.

"And you want him?" he asked more quietly.

"Yes," I said, just as quietly.

"And Alex?" he demanded.

I shrugged at that. "I haven't spoken to him. I don't know if he even wants to be with me anymore, never mind as a part of..." I gestured around me as I didn't know what to call it.

"So right now..."

"Right now, I want to be with you and Lachlan," I said firmly, so that there could be no doubt.

"Then I will try," he said. "For you, I will try."

I beamed at him. "That's all I ask," I said and pulled him to me to kiss him, but we were interrupted by the elevator doors opening. We both looked over. My heart sped up as I saw Lachlan step out. I took him in, seeing just how gorgeous he was.

"Hey," he said and stopped near the coffee table.

He looked at Rex, who looked back at him in earnest.

"You told him then," Lachlan said.

"Yes," I replied. "We have decided to try." I couldn't help the huge grin that appeared on my face.

Lachlan's eyes lit up, but then he looked at Rex with a raised eyebrow.

Rex avoided his gaze for a moment, but then looked him squarely in the eye. "I am doing this for Cassandra," he said. "Whatever fantasy you have of me, isn't going to happen."

Lachlan just shrugged as if he didn't really care one way or the other and took off his leather jacket. He sauntered over to us and took me in his arms, dragging me to him as he claimed my mouth in one of the finest kisses I had ever had. He slid his tongue into my mouth, pushing against mine with a gentleness that made my knees weak. He withdrew it and gave it back to me in an intoxicating rhythm. He was fucking my mouth with his tongue and it made me crave him. I needed him to make love to me, I needed to see if it would be as good as I was imagining it as he kissed me.

Without a word, he started to unbutton my blouse and then pushed it off my shoulders to pool on the floor. He pulled back and glanced down with a smirk.

"Cotton?" he laughed.

I heard Rex stifle his snort of amusement at my expense.

"Hey," I said haughtily. "If I had expected a sexy tryst when I got home, I would've worn something less comfortable."

Rex, reached out to flick the bra clasp, undoing it with ease. "I like it," he murmured, and turned me around to lower his mouth to mine.

It was only the second time we had kissed, but it was incredible. I was flying high sandwiched between these two men. One kissed me with such a forcefully passion I wanted weep with joy. The other reached around to my nipples. He twisted them just hard enough to elicit a yelp from me, then he kissed the back of my neck and snaked his hands lower.

Lachlan undid my skirt and it fell forgotten to the floor. He twanged my sensible cotton panties with a chuckle. He gripped them tightly and suddenly ripped them from me, causing me to cry out in pain as the material bit into me.

Rex picked me up and carried me a few steps forward, but then stopped.

"This way," Lachlan said, taking Rex by the elbow and leading him to my bedroom.

"Yes," I breathed out as Rex glanced down at me for confirmation.

He placed me gently down on the corner of the bed, then he stripped off his jacket and boots. He glanced at Lachlan in discomfort. Lachlan had already peeled off his jeans and was commando beneath them. My eyes widened at the enormous erection that bounced around in front of him. I licked my lips, desperate to get it in my mouth and suck him until he came.

He must've seen it written all over my face. "Naughty girl," he murmured, his eyes hooded with desire.

"What are you going to do about it?" I asked seductively.

"Spank you," he replied in a sexy tone that made my pussy clench.

I cast my glance at Rex, who watched us silently. "Come here," I said, holding out my hand to him.

He came closer. I sat up and undid his jeans, hooking my fingers into the sides and pulling them down slowly. I already knew he wouldn't have anything else on underneath. I licked my lips again. His cock sprung free, already rock-hard. I couldn't stop myself from taking him in my mouth. I heard Lachlan moan from a few feet away, enjoying watching me suck Rex off. He climbed on the bed next to me and trailed his fingers down my stomach until he reached my clit.

"You sure?" he asked quietly, holding his hand still. "There's no going back after this."

I removed my mouth from Rex and whispered, "I'm sure."

He didn't hesitate after that, flicking my clit with his fingers, before he pushed me back to the bed and spread my legs. He ducked his head and lowered his mouth to me, plunging his tongue straight into me. I cried out as he tongue fucked me so expertly, I thought I might die of ecstasy. His thumb circled my clit as his tongue worked furiously to bring me to an orgasm that made me scream so loudly, I thought the whole city could hear me.

"Fuck, Cassie," he murmured. He raised his mouth to mine. I could taste myself on his lips. "You are divine."

He kissed me passionately, but I pulled away, lacing my fingers through Rex's. I dragged him onto the bed with us.

"Kiss me," I demanded.

Without any hesitation, he swooped down on me, his tongue lapping at my lips, before he plunged it into my mouth.

Lachlan's fingers entered me, thrusting in and out, making me shudder again in Rex's arms.

Rex pulled away and looked at me questioningly.

"Say it," I said. I thought I knew what he wanted.

"I don't want to play with you tonight, Cassandra," he said. "I want it to be different."

"Me too," I replied, knowing that the three of us had all the time in the world to experience all the things we could do with one another.

Lachlan moved me into a position on the bed which left me in no doubt as to what he wanted to do. He knelt behind me, leaning over me to push my head towards Rex's cock again. I took him in my mouth, sucking him, licking every inch of him as he slid his hand into my hair.

"Oh, yes," Lachlan whispered and thrust hard into me. He waited a few seconds before he pulled back and then did it again. And again. I was aroused to the point of no return. I came, pulsing around his cock and that's when he started to pound into me. He grabbed my hips painfully and slammed into me, pulling all the way back out before slamming into me again.

"Fuck," I cried, releasing my hold on Rex as I shook with another orgasm that raced through my body with such heat, I felt like I was on fire.

Lachlan groaned loudly but withdrew before he came and lay down next to me. He gave me a smoldering look as I fell back. I dragged Rex on top of me.

I wrapped my legs around him, not giving him the chance to escape.

"Take me," I whispered, tilting my hips up.

He gave me what I wanted, but with a pained whimper, keeping his eyes tightly closed.

"Look at me," I demanded.

He opened his eyes as he slid all the way inside me. I knew it was because Lachlan had got to me first. I didn't want to give him time to think about it, so I rolled us over. I rode him hard and fast, bringing forth my own orgasm before he grabbed my nipples and tweaked them painfully hard with a growl.

"Easy, tiger," Lachlan said to him, pulling Rex's hands away and replacing them with his own. He rubbed my nipples with his palms, then he lowered his head and took one in his mouth. He bit down gently and rolled it between his teeth.

"Oooh!" I cried out as sensation after sensation hit me. I came around Rex's cock again, pulsating intensely. It was enough for him to release into me, jerking his hips up as he came forcefully with his eyes on mine.

I climbed off him and lowered my head, taking Lachlan's enormous shaft into my mouth with a soft moan. He groaned and threw his head back, fisting his hand tightly into my hair. He held my head in place as he fucked my mouth, gently at first, but then with more vigor as he grew closer to his orgasm. Rex reached over to circle my clit. I writhed on the bed. I needed him to please me. He didn't disappointment me and soon I was shaking again.

Lachlan dragged his cock out of my mouth and pushed me back to the bed. He grabbed my ankles and raised my legs straight up into the air. He pressed his cock at my tight entrance and thrust into me quickly. He came almost instantly, shooting his load with a grunt. He let go of my legs and fell on top of me to kiss me. He rolled off and watched as Rex dipped his fingers into me and swirled them around. He removed them and pressed them to my lips, making me taste their combined cum. It made Lachlan groan in ecstasy. He leaned over and clasped his fingers around Rex's.

Rex's eyes went straight to his as he tried to pull back, but Lachlan held him firmly. He brought their hands up to his mouth to lick the remainder off Rex's fingers.

"Jesus," I whimpered as a bolt of lust shot through me with such force, I nearly came on the spot.

"Turned on, Sweetcheeks?" Lachlan smirked at me. "Just wait."

I half expected Rex to yank his hand back after that remark, but he didn't. He let Lachlan hold it, and even let him stroke his face with his other hand.

"You have two people here who care about you," Lachlan whispered to him. "Let us."

He nodded, his eyes on mine.

In that moment, I knew that this was right.

I thought briefly of Alex and I hoped that one day he could get passed his anger and join us.

TWENTY-EIGHT

~Rex~

I watched Cassie as she slept.

Cassie.

I tried it out, whispering it in the dark. She had muttered to me, as I wished her good night, to call her Cassie. It suited her better than Cassandra. I rolled onto my back and stared at the ceiling. I couldn't believe that I was lying here in this bed with her and Lachlan. He was curled up around her as he slept, and it didn't bother me. I thought that it would. It had definitely bothered me when I saw him fucking her, but only for a few minutes. Then she had included me, and I forgot to be jealous. It was perfect. She was happy and that was the only thing that I wanted. I could put my own discomfort aside to see her as happy as she was last night, in her bed with me and Lachlan. She was the only thing that mattered.

I wondered where this left Alex? She hadn't mentioned

if she had broken up with him, but I assume that had to be the case now.

But as usual, the dark cloud came overhead and rained on my happiness.

It wasn't perfect. It was a lie. I didn't belong in this pure, white bed. I belonged in the pit with the rest of the sinners. Try as I might, I couldn't leave her, though. Not before and certainly not now. She turned in her sleep and snuggled into me. I ached to tell her about me, but I knew there wasn't a single part of her that would accept me, so I would live the lie just so I could be with her. I stroked her back, sleep as far away from me as it usually was, but I must have drifted off at some point, because I awoke suddenly, in terror.

Cassie wasn't in my arms. Where was she? Had she found out about me and left? I sat up. My breathing slowed as I saw her curled up in a ball under the covers in Lachlan's arms again. I scooted over and folded myself against her back, wrapping my arms around her. She shuffled and turned into my chest. I relaxed. She was safe and she was...ours.

I looked over her at Lachlan, sound asleep. I cautiously moved my hand over to his and gripped it tightly. It was as far as I could go right now, but I wanted him to know that I cared about him too.

I looked at the clock and it was only 2 A.M. I didn't think I would sleep again for fear of waking up alone, so I just held her, and we lay entwined around each other until her alarm went off at six.

~Cassie~

I STRETCHED and blinked sleepily at Rex. "Hi," I said with a slow smile.

"Morning," he said as he leaned over and turned the alarm off. I took the opportunity to kiss his glorious chest. He chuckled and bent down to kiss my lips. I looked around for Lachlan and found him fast asleep on the edge of the bed on my other side.

"Did you sleep well?" I asked Rex. He nodded evasively and asked, "Did you?"

"The best," I said, and I meant it. I had felt so safe and protected; like I'd had two guardian angels watching over me. I had been free to crash like I hadn't done in a long time.

"Good," he said and kissed my nose. "Coffee?"

"Mm, please," I said and watched him get up. He pulled his jeans on.

I shook my head. "Uh-uh."

He turned to me, puzzled. I nearly drooled at the sight of him. His angel wing tattoos were on full display just above his open jeans. He was the sexiest thing I had ever seen.

"No pants allowed," I said, wagging my finger at him.

"Oh?" he asked as he unashamedly removed them anyway.

"Good boy," I murmured and then watched his very sexy, naked ass as he sauntered out of the bedroom. I stretched again and smiled as Lachlan woke up.

"Hi," he said, leaning over to kiss my nose.

"Hi," I replied, looking down shyly. The things we did last night had definitely moved us past the friend zone. It was unchartered territory.

"Cas?"

I looked up at him. His handsome face was full of concern.

"Everything okay?" he asked warily.

"Yes, I'm...we've..." I huffed out a breath. "Done stuff..." I added lamely.

"No shit," he said with a laugh. "And I fucking enjoyed it. I love you, Cassie. I adore you."

I smiled and relaxed. It wasn't weird. It was perfect. "I fucking enjoyed it too," I laughed and linked my fingers through his. "Rex is making coffee."

"He's a god!" Lachlan exclaimed and leapt out of bed, sauntering out of the bedroom completely naked as well.

I bit my lip and slipped into the bathroom quickly before I pulled on my robe and went to join them.

They were talking, or at least Lachlan was regaling Rex with a tale and Rex was listening intently while he went about making breakfast.

I loved seeing them there in my kitchen. It just seemed right.

"Don't be a hypocrite, Cassie," Rex reprimanded me, strolling over and undoing the belt on me robe. "Fair's fair."

I grinned and let the robe fall to the floor. I enjoyed his look of desire and seeing his body react to my nakedness. Before I knew what hit me, Lachlan had swept me up in his strong arms, wrapping my legs around him as he impaled me on his cock, standing right there in the middle of the kitchen. I gasped with surprise, but the act was so fucking hot. I creamed his cock as I gripped his shoulders tightly, riding him fiercely to our utter satisfaction. He unloaded into me with a grunt and then placed me on the counter. The granite was cold against my ass, but I soon heated it up. My body lit up when Rex took his turn with me, lifting me off the counter and lowering me to the floor to fuck me hard and fast. We came together, our cries of desire echoing around us. Lachlan was watching, his breathing heavy.

"You will have to let us take you together. Soon," he stated and then poured us a cup of coffee each as he let that sink in.

I glanced at Rex. He nodded his consent so all that was left was for me to say. "Okay, soon." I stood up with a gulp. Taking them together was a huge step. It would connect us in a way that I hoped we were ready for. I had never done it before, so I hoped one of them had so they knew what the hell to do with the tangle we were bound to end up in. As I pictured it, I got all aroused again and made my excuses before I took them like that right there in my kitchen, when I should have been getting ready for work.

"Go and get showered now and breakfast will be ready when you get out," Rex said, also getting to his feet.

I nodded and he added. "I will drive you to work today."

Lachlan cleared his throat.

"*We* will drive you to work today," he amended with a smile.

I returned the smile and disappeared into the bedroom only to return with a frown a moment later. "Did you find out anything about that person who has been calling me?"

Lachlan looked up curiously. "What person?"

"Untraceable," Rex said, shaking his head, ignoring Lachlan. "I was going to tell you last night, but things went in a different direction."

I snorted and said, "Hm, just a slightly different direction. So, there's nothing I can do?"

"You can let me worry about it," he said.

I bit the inside of my lip, only worried that he couldn't find anything out. Maybe it was time to bring in the police.

I heard Lachlan ask again. Rex answered him that time, but I just wanted to shower and forget about it.

———

FIFTEEN MINUTES LATER, I walked back into my bedroom to find Lachlan on the bed, glaring at me as he shoved his feet into his pants. "You should have told me," he barks at me.

"It's nothing," I said brushing it off.

"Nothing?" he spat out. "Oh no. You don't get to go all 'Cassie' on this one. This is serious. They are calling you *at home*. I will get to the bottom of this. No one threatens my woman and gets away with it!"

Rex cleared his throat. He was leaning against the door frame, still naked, with his arms crossed.

"*Our* woman," Lachlan amended. "Until this is sorted out, you will be with one or both of us 24/7. Are we clear?"

I inwardly smiled. He had gone all caveman on me, and I liked it. I was used to dealing with shit on my own. I didn't mind it, but this made me feel so special and so loved I wanted to weep. I nodded, close to tears. He gathered me to him, mistaking my tears for worried ones.

"We won't let anything happen to you," he crooned to me.

"I know," I told him. "I'm not worried. I know you will protect me. Both of you."

"Damn straight," Lachlan said, letting me go. "Now get dressed so we can drive you to work. We will see you at lunchtime and then be back to collect you after work.

"Don't you have jobs to go to?" I asked, lightly.

"Oh, please," Lachlan said but gave Rex a look that I didn't understand. Rex didn't like it and stood up straight, his face closing down completely. I wanted to question it, but I was running late. It could wait until later. Granddaddy was pissed enough at me, without me aggravating the situation by turning up late.

AFTER BEING force-fed some breakfast by Rex, I was driven to work in Lachlan's SUV. I was blown away with this. It had all happened so quickly in spite of our previous relationships. I was happy and relaxed. They were taking care of me in a way that no one ever had before. I could definitely get used to this.

Lachlan pulled up outside the office and kissed me goodbye. "See you at lunch," he said in a tone that warned me not to argue with him.

Rex climbed out of the back and opened the door for me. He leaned down to kiss me softly. "See you later," he whispered and then jumped into the seat I'd vacated and they both watched me as I turned and walked into the building.

~Alex~

I STOPPED dead on the sidewalk and nearly lost my coffee. I watched Rex help Cassie out of a black SUV. My stomach clenched as I saw them kiss. I frowned as Rex got back in the passenger side and saw then that the driver was Lachlan. I should have known, should have been expecting it, but it still hurt like a bitch to see her with Rex. I should be happy for her, that she was with someone who could give her what she wanted, something that I knew I was incapable of giving her. But the bitterness of the bile in my throat was disgusting. I gripped my briefcase and strode forward into the building.

Cassie had moved on. I was alone and the woman I loved wasn't who I thought she was.

I got to my desk and was in the worst mood ever. It was a few hours before someone dared to speak to me, and I took their head off. I felt bad and was going to apologize to Nancy, when my phone rang. It was the call I had been waiting for. I breathed in deeply, plastered a smile on my face and answered the important call.

AFTER WORK, Rex was waiting for her, leaning up against the massive, black SUV. I watched as he swooped down to give her a kiss. It made me feel sick. I was furious at the blatant display of affection. It was a slap in the face, as if our relationship had meant nothing.

I fingered the envelope that was in my jacket pocket. I'd wanted to leave it in her office on my way out but changed my mind in case I ran into her. I decided to drop it off very early in the morning before she came in.

I turned to head towards the subway with a sigh.

"Alex?" a man's voice called out to me.

I stopped and looked over my shoulder. It was that friend of Cassie's, Lachlan. I saw the SUV speed off behind him. I focused on him, wondering that he wanted.

"I need to talk to you," he said, more than a little annoyed.

"What about?" I asked rudely.

"What do you think?" he snapped at me. He grabbed my elbow and steered me out of the crowds into a quieter space.

"Look, if Cassandra sent you here, I'm..."

"She didn't. She doesn't know I'm here," he said.

I gritted my teeth.

"You need to talk to her," Lachlan said. "Whether it be for closure, or to sort out your issues, you need to let her in. She is upset and it is making me upset. You don't want me upset." He glowered at me and I believed him.

"I don't know what to say," I said with a shrug. "She isn't the woman I thought she was..."

Lachlan gave me a piercing stare, but then understanding crossed his face. "Oh, you're one of those."

"What is 'one of those'?" I asked, offended by his tone.

"A judgmental asshole," he said matter-of-factly.

"I beg your pardon," I said. "How dare you."

"But you are, just because she likes a bit of fun. Don't knock it till you've tried it," he interrupted.

"No, thank you. I have had quite the experience in that area, and it is not for me," I said stiffly and carried on walking.

"She isn't into anything hardcore, you know. You should speak to her, ask her what she likes," Lachlan said slyly.

I felt myself blushing. I wasn't a prude, I knew I wasn't, but Lachlan was discussing this so casually I sure as shit felt like one.

He grabbed my arm again and we stopped walking. "Don't you want her back?"

I didn't answer him because I didn't know. I couldn't give her what she wanted, and I couldn't be with a woman who wanted *that*.

"It isn't about pain and whips and chains, Alex," Lachlan said softly. "It is about what you can do with these." He linked his fingers through mine and held our joined hands up. I snatched mine back quickly. "And these," he said and ran his fingers lightly over my lips. "And this." He tapped my temple. I jerked back from this intimacy with a fierce frown.

"What do you mean?" I asked confused.

"Creativity and imagination," he whispered. "Close your eyes, picture Cassie blindfolded. Picture yourself standing over her. She has no idea where you are or what you are going to do to her next. She has no idea if you will touch her, kiss her, or leave her waiting."

Oh God. I gulped. I could definitely picture that, and it was most pleasing.

"See," he said and smirked at me.

I cleared my throat. "But I have seen what she has done to him," I said quietly.

Lachlan looked up sharply.

I explained. "We go to the same gym. He prefers to work out shirtless."

"Ah," he says. "Look, I don't know the ins and outs of that, but I do know what Cassie likes. If you could speak to her, tell her you would be willing to try, you could work it out."

"How do you know that?" I asked. "She seems pretty happy with tall, dark, and brooding."

"And the rest," he murmured, confusing me even more. "Wouldn't you always wonder, if you didn't try?" he coaxed.

Yeah, I would. Before I found out about Rex, I thought I was falling in love with her. I also thought that she felt the same. I frowned as I remembered that she had given up on us after only four days. I didn't stop to think that I had given up on her first by storming out and not letting her explain. I nodded but remained silent.

"Look," Lachlan said, "The thing about Cassie is, she has serious abandonment issues. There hasn't been a single person in her life that hasn't left her at some point. She is fragile and in need of people who love her. Do you love her?"

I just stared him. Fragile? That didn't sound like Cassie. "Yes, I love her," I said eventually.

"Then go to her. Tonight."

"No, I can't. I don't know what to say to her."

"Whatever it is that is on your mind. She wants to talk to you; she has things she needs to say. She cares about you and I want her to be happy."

I frowned at him again. He was speaking like he was in love with her. Not that it would surprise me. She was one hell of a woman. "I'll think about it," I said.

"The gesture will go miles, Alex. Show her that not everyone leaves her. Show her that you love her."

"It's not that easy. I can't accept what she is."

"She is a woman, not a fucking monster, you prick," he suddenly snarls at me, and then visibly calms himself.

"I know that," I grit out, getting pissed off with this asshole. What's it to him anyway if I speak to Cassie or not?

"I have a lot invested in her happiness. Just speak to her."

He stalked off, leaving my mind reeling.

One thing was clear though. I needed to talk to Cassie. Clear the air. Whatever happened after that, well, we would have to wait and see.

TWENTY-NINE

~Cassie~

I stalked into my office the next day, slightly put-out. I'd heard from Marjorie not a moment ago, that Alex was waiting for me.

"What do you want?" I asked him rudely.

He looked startled. "I, uh," he said, faltering. He blinked at me as I stood there glaring at him.

"Speak or get out," I said as I tore my eyes from his and thumped my briefcase on my desk. I couldn't stand to look at him, remembering the disgust I'd seen in his eyes less than a week ago.

"Cass..." he started.

"That's *Ms. Bellingham* to you," I said haughtily.

He flinched. "I'll come back," he muttered and backed towards the door.

"I'm sorry, Alex. Please sit down and say what it is you

came here for." I felt bad for being so bitchy to him, but I wanted him to know I was still so hurt by his actions.

He sat and twiddled his thumbs for a moment. "We need to talk, Cassie. Not here, not now, but I want to clear the air and apologize to you for running out the way I did."

I looked at him. What was I supposed to do about that? "I'm with Rex now...and Lachlan, it doesn't matter," I said and waited for his reaction to that news.

I watched as his eyebrows went skyward and then slammed back down into a fierce frown. "Oh?" he asked coldly.

"Look, I'm not explaining myself to you here. If you still want to talk, I'll come over later." There, it was up to him to decide what to do now. If he declined, then at least we had some closure.

"Uh...okay," he said after a minute.

I could see the thoughts racing through his head. His questions, his pain, his anger, but he kept it together, probably only because we were at work. But I wanted him to know. Wanted to see if there was any chance, he would accept it. I doubted it though judging by the look on his face.

"Come straight from work. I'll make us dinner," he said. He stood up quickly and left before I could decline his offer.

"Great," I muttered and leaned back in my chair. "I'll be there," I added to the closed door.

I thought of nothing else but the meeting for the rest of the day. I was a complete disaster. Granddaddy had made a big mistake in giving me his company. I was in no state to run downstairs, never mind run a global corporation.

I sighed. At the very least, going to see Alex might make me feel better about his reasons for running out on me. I had to admit I was wildly curious. It had to be more than just about Rex. If it had been, he wouldn't have invited me over for dinner to talk about it. He would have left it once he found out we were together. Adding Lachlan into the mix, must've thrown him. He is probably more confused now than he was earlier. I felt guilty about the way I launched it at him. I should've been more thoughtful.

~Alex~

I WATCHED Cassie climb into her car. I was relieved that Rex *and Lachlan* hadn't turned up to collect her. Man, that was a kick in the gut I hadn't been expecting. It made me think twice about this. Firstly, she was into all that stuff and now she was hooking up with *two* men. How the fuck does that even work? I gulped as the mental image was not one to my liking.

The guys not being here must mean that she was still coming over to my apartment. I wanted to call and cancel, but it wouldn't solve anything. I still wanted to tell her what my issue was with her lifestyle. I hailed a cab and asked him to step on it. I arrived home about five minutes before she rang the doorbell. I buzzed her up and told her to come straight in. I quickly pulled out the ingredients for a simple pasta sauce. I was chopping and frying when she pushed the door open and stepped in cautiously before she closed it.

Cassie stayed by the door, looking awkward and inse-cure. I knew without a doubt that I loved her. I didn't care what kinky shit she was into. I loved her and I would tell her that as soon as I could open my mouth and make words come out. I didn't know what to make of the other two guys. It was something I would have to hear from her once I told her what *I* was feeling. My mouth was dry, and my onions were burning, but I didn't take my eyes off her.

She rolled hers and stepped forward. "Are you trying to burn the building down? Some apology that would be," she said and flicked off the gas.

"Sorry," I muttered and fanned the air. My eyes were watering and so were hers, so I took her hand and led her out of the kitchen.

"For what?" she asked. "Trying to kill me or for running out on me?"

"Both," I said, letting go of her hand. We both sat on the sofa. I turned to her. It was now or never. "Cassie, I was such an ass. I was hurt and disappointed and there are some things I need to explain to you that will hopefully make you see why I did what I did," I said.

"Okay," she said and settled down to hear me out.

That was good. At least she was prepared to listen to my story.

"Wine first," I said and got up to get us both a glass. I then launched into my tale in graphic detail as to why I just couldn't accept that way of life.

~Cassie~

I BLINKED at him as he finished speaking and took it all in. "I see," I said. "You think that I am some sort of whip-wielding child molester?"

"What? God, no! Cassie. I just have trouble accepting it when people do things, I am not comfortable with. I associate that type of behavior with what my mother did to that poor kid. I can't see the difference." He dropped his head into his hands. "I know I am making such a mess of this."

I stayed silent, trying to process what he had just said. I completely understood his disgust. What his mother did was inexcusable, disgusting, outrageous! But I was *nothing* like that. I had to get him to see that. "I'm not like that," I said quietly.

"I know you aren't. Not exactly, but I saw what you did to him," Alex said just as quietly.

I drew in a deep breath. "Excuse me?" I asked.

Alex sighed. "We go to the same gym. I have seen the marks that you have left on him."

"Oh," I said and chewed my lip. "Let me explain."

"There is no need, you like what you like. I'm just...I'm sorry for judging you, that was wrong. But that aside, Cassie, you still hurt me by not telling me about him. You said you were going to go on the occasional date to keep up appearances. You never said you had someone you were still sleeping with."

I shook my head vehemently. "No, Alex. I wasn't with him when we were together." I knew I wasn't telling the whole truth and was about to add more when he interrupted.

"But he said on that Friday you were expecting him. You don't have social calls at ten at night."

"I know. I was seeing him up until I decided to give us a

chance. He left the country for work before I got a chance to tell him and he just assumed our arrangement was still the same when he came back. That's the truth, Alex."

"Okay, but what about Lachlan?" he asked.

I knew it was coming, but I was still unprepared for the question.

"I don't see how you can be with two different men," he said when I remained silent. "They might be all chummy and okay with that, but I don't see it as acceptable."

Ouch. I needed to explain it to him, that it wasn't what he thought it was.

"I get that, Alex, but it's not entirely what you think. I *am* seeing both of them, but we are in a relationship. Together." I let that sink in. His face went ashen and he licked his lips. I carried on before he could comment. "Lachlan came to me a few days before you met him at my apartment. He told me that he loved me and that he wanted to be with me. He also said that he had feelings for Rex and that, if I wanted it, I should find a way to make it work. I told him about you, and he accepted that you would also be involved."

"What?" he spluttered, turning red in the face as his eyes bugged out. "Cassandra! How..."

"Don't judge," I snapped at him. "It is what I want. I want to be loved and taken care of. I want to be everything to someone, as they are to me. Why would I choose when I have two men who are all that and more? Why *should* I?"

He shook his head at me. "I love you, Cassie," he blurted out. "I thought, before all of this, that you were starting to feel the same."

"I was. I wanted to speak to you, but you wouldn't answer my calls," I said.

"So, you just gave up and went to them instead," Alex said bitterly.

"It wasn't like that," I said quietly. "I have explained it to you the best way that I can."

"I get it. They give you what you need. You can go out in public with them. You can introduce them to your family. All the things that you can't do with me." He sounded angry, but I didn't blame him.

"I don't know what to say," I said at a loss. I was confused. He said he got it, but did that mean he accepted it; however, it wasn't for him, or that he wanted to be a part of it? I knew I still wanted him. I knew that Lachlan was on board with bringing him in. Rex might need a bit more convincing.

"The ball is in your court," I said eventually. "If you love me and want to be with me, then you have to accept that I come with Rex and Lachlan now. I understand if it is something that you can't agree to, then we should part ways now."

He gave me a serious look. "You really expect me to join you in this...three-way relationship?" His disbelief was evident.

"I want you to. Whether you do is up to you, Alex."

He just stared at me.

I stood up. "I should leave. Think about what I said. If I don't hear from you by the end of the week, I won't bother you again." With that said, I ran from his apartment, out into the night, with tears streaming down my face. I knew I had lost him. He wouldn't accept it. I could tell already that I wouldn't hear from him.

~Lachlan~

I STRODE into Cassie's apartment and faced off with Rex. "We need to talk." He was tidying up but stopped at my tone. I narrowed my eyes at him.

"I let the housekeeper go," Rex said, straightening up. "Ella was the stalker."

"What?" I yelled at him. "I will kill her!"

"Or do you expect me to do it?" Rex asked, his face cold.

"You know?"

"*You* know?"

"I do," I said. I paused then as I realized what he'd said. "*Was* the stalker?"

Rex nodded once. "I had words with her. Let's just say that she won't be bothering Cassie anymore."

"Meaning?"

"Meaning, I told her I would kill her if she so much as breathed in Cassie's direction again," Rex snapped.

"Did she say why?" I was losing sight of this conversation and Rex was losing his patience with me, but I needed to know.

"Jealousy of Cassie's life, but it was exacerbated by the fact that she was dating Alex and he broke up with her to be with Cassie. She only meant to scare her."

"Ooh," I said, taking that in. "But she's dealt with? For sure?"

"Yes!" he yelled at me "Are you going to tell Cassie what you know?"

I regarded him. He seemed confident that Ella wasn't going to hassle Cassie again. He was truly only concerned that I was going to tell her who he really was. Not that I would turn him in. Or the dire consequences if I did.

"No," I said after a pause. "However, I expect you to quit, or resign, or whatever it is that you do."

"Already have," Rex said.

Okay, this conversation wasn't half as awkward I thought it would be.

"Good. You need to be a decent man for Cassie. I know you can be. I will help you. I *want* to help you get over your past, Rex. I want you to open up. You don't have to tell Cassie anything yet, and I won't betray your trust, but she will ask eventually. This relationship is for the long-haul and she will expect answers. I will help you get to a place where you can give them to her without flipping out or running away."

"You can't expect me to tell her about my former employment," Rex said, the desperation filtering in now that I have laid it out for him.

"No, I don't expect that. She would run a mile if she ever found out about that. Especially in light of Richard Pomfries IV."

I saw Rex gulp. "How do you know the details?"

"Do you know who the Captain is?" I asked him.

Rex blinked at me. "Do you?"

"Yes. He is Cassie's Uncle Teddy." I dropped that bombshell and waited for it to sink in.

"What?" he choked out.

"Yep. I have been associating with him as I had my suspicions about him for a while now. I wanted to make sure that Cassie was nowhere near anything shady. Turns out, Uncle Teddy is as shady as they come."

"So am I," Rex pointed out.

"Yes, but you would never hurt her. I know that."

"Are you sure about that?" he challenged. "I kill innocent people. Killed," he amended quickly.

I gave him a puzzled look. "Innocents? They weren't innocent, Rex." I pulled the file out of the back of my pants and slung it on the coffee table. I knew Cassie wasn't due home yet, but I needed to get this conversation to a conclusion, soon.

"What do you know?" he demanded.

"What do *you* know?"

"Nothing," he spat out. "Don't ask, don't tell."

"Hmm, probably better that way. Teddy's wife, Rebecca, was killed seven years ago by a drunk driver. Do you remember that?"

"Yes, vaguely. The Bellingham family were outraged because the driver had got away with it on a technicality."

"Alan James," I said as his eyes found mine. I saw the pieces fall into place.

"The name of my first target." He frantically grabbed my hands, crushing them. "More," he demanded.

I dragged my hands out of Rex's. I couldn't believe that he didn't know that every target he had taken out wasn't an innocent victim. They were all criminals who had fallen through the cracks of the law for one reason or another. I had it all memorized, so I went through them all one by one for him.

"Killers," he said flatly. "They were all killers."

"Do you see now?" I asked. "You have given the families of those innocent victims the justice that they deserve."

"Do you really believe that?" he asked. "Can you really forgive everything I have done just because the targets weren't innocents themselves?"

"Yes," I said. "You think of Cassie as your redemption, and maybe she is. But I can be that for you as well. I can help you be the man I know you think she deserves. You wouldn't have quit if you didn't think that already."

"Why do you care about me?" he asked, his eyes so serious I wanted to hold him.

"I see your pain. I don't understand it yet, but I know it must have been a fucked-up childhood." I took a chance and stroked his face. He let me. Just barely. "Let me help you," I whispered to him, dying to kiss him, but knowing he wasn't ready for that. Maybe one day.

He nodded slowly, relinquishing his control and offering up his trust to me.

I did lean over then to kiss him softly. He accepted it but didn't encourage it. "I won't let you down," I murmured to him.

"Neither will I," he whispered back.

———

~Alex~

I CLIMBED out of the shower and dried off. I was still reeling over everything that Cassie had said to me last night. My eyes felt like grit as I had fallen asleep with my contacts in last night. I rubbed at them and then rooted around my nightstand drawer for my glasses. I hated them, but I couldn't see without them, so I shoved them up my nose. I flattened my damp hair and made for the kitchen for hot coffee, only to stop dead halfway there. Rex was sitting casually in my armchair.

Shit. "Rex," I started as I slowly lifted my hands. If he was going to start throwing punches, I wanted to be ready.

"Alex," Rex replied coldly. "Want to explain what the fuck is going on with my girlfriend."

I shook my head. "You need to speak to Cassie. I don't know what she is thinking."

"I know she came here last night and when she got home, she was in tears." He stood up and took a menacing step forward. "What did you do to her?"

"Nothing!" I exclaimed. "She explained about your... relationship." I stopped speaking then. I had no idea if Cassie had mentioned to Rex about wanting me to join their little circle. A decision I still hadn't decided on. Most of me was sure it wasn't for me, even though I loved her. But...*I loved her*. If it was the only way to be with her, then a small part of me wanted it.

"And?" Rex glowered at me.

"Not up to me to say," I said shortly. I wasn't getting involved in this for all the world. "You need to speak to Cassie," I reiterated.

"Oh, I will," Rex said. "I'm asking you first."

I did not like his tone one bit and said, "If you hurt her..."

Rex snorted at him. "I won't hurt *her*," he scoffed. "I love her. She made me feel something again. I owe her everything. You on the other hand, if you hurt her in any way..."

"Look, Rex," I interrupted. "I don't want to get in the middle of this."

Rex stood up and then eyed me curiously. He moved closer. He tilted his head. "You look different. Familiar," he said, almost to himself. "Do I know you from before?"

"What?" I asked. "No, I don't think so. We met at the gym..."

"No," Rex said and shook his head and the blood drained from his face. "It's you."

"What?"

"Where are you from?" Rex barked at me.

"New...New Jersey," I stammered.

"Where exactly?"

I stuttered out my mother's address and Rex's face hardened. "You don't remember me?"

I shook his head. What the fuck is going on?

"You helped me," Rex whispered. "You saved me."

"What?" I asked again.

"Nine years ago, the basement, the kid you let go..." Rex pressed.

All the blood drained from my face as well. "You?" I croaked out. "No, that kid was..."

Rex grimaced. "Me," he said.

"Motherfucker," I said as I lowered my hands and bent over, catching my breath.

"Yeah," Rex agreed, huffing out his breath.

"You got out? You got away from him?" I asked after a few moments.

"Who, Jerry?" Rex asked.

"The bald guy, built like a brick shithouse."

"Yeah, Jerry. Yeah I did."

"Jerry," I said. "Lucky you," I added quietly.

Rex's eyes found mine sharply. "He hurt you? He hurt you for letting me go?"

I straightened up, not wanting to relive the worst humiliation, the worst *moment* of my life with this guy of all people.

"Did he hurt you?" Rex demanded.

I nodded stiffly, beyond mortified.

"I killed him," Rex growled. "I killed him and my whore of a mother."

I looked at him in surprise, but then not really, because who was I kidding? I probably would have as well had I been capable, and Rex looked more than capable. I nodded briskly, looking away wondering if Cassie knew about this.

Rex pulled a gun out of the back of his pants. "If you say one word to her..." he warned.

I choked back my fear. I shook my head vehemently. "She won't hear it from me," I said quickly.

Rex glowered at me, not believing me. I seriously feared for my life in that moment. He was one scary-ass motherfucker.

"I swear," I said. "No one will ever hear it from me. It goes to the grave."

Somehow, he decided to believe me that time and shoved the gun into the back of his pants. He straightened his leather jacket out.

"There is something going on with the two of you and I want to know what it is," he said. "I am going to speak to Cassie and if I don't like what she says, I will be back."

I just nodded. What else could I do? If he decided that he didn't want me as a part of their circle, I was a goner. I gulped loudly.

Rex disappeared quickly, slamming the door behind him.

I stared after him.

Shit! I couldn't believe that the scared teenager in my mother's basement turned out to be Rex. Fuck, talk about a small world.

THIRTY

~Alex~

Another day passed without me making a decision about Cassie's offer. Every time I thought I had decided, I changed my mind. One of my biggest concerns was how would it work? Would she want to be with all of us together? That meant that things would get seen, touched, accidentally or otherwise. The other one, and this was massive, was how was I supposed to stand there and watch her fucking not one other guy, but *two*. And would either of them want to fuck *me*, because that was a deal breaker. That is what made me change my mind every time I thought I could go through with it.

One thing was clear, Rex hadn't returned to kill me, so I assumed he was on board with this plan, or, Cassie simply hadn't told him yet.

I went over it all in my head again. Tried to picture the

four of us on her bed together and *what* would go *where*. How she would look with Rex's body joined with hers? What would her face look like when she came from Lachlan's efforts? What if I was sub-par and struggled to get her to orgasm while the other two managed in a few seconds?

"ARGH!" I punched the wall. This was getting me nowhere. There was only one fucking way to answer these questions and that was to dive in headfirst. Take a fucking risk for once in my life. If it didn't work out and I had to leave, then at least I knew I had given it a try.

I glanced at the clock. It was late, nearing midnight. But I had to do this now, or I would chicken out.

I raced out of my apartment and hailed a cab about half a mile down the road. I gave him Cassie's address and told him to get a move on. When he pulled up, I threw a fifty at him and jumped out without waiting for change. I didn't want it. I just wanted to get to Cassie and tell her I was in. I rushed through the doors to her building and got stopped immediately by a burly looking security guard that was clearly there to deter weirdos like me in the middle of night.

I glanced at his nametag and smiled at him. "Pete. I am here to see Ms. Bellingham. Penthouse."

Pete gave me a suspicious look but obliged me and pressed the buzzer.

As I waited, it pissed me off that Rex seemed to be able to come and go into her place as he chose. That would have to be discussed. I wouldn't stand here like, how did Lachlan put it? Oh yes, *the help*, while Rex flashed his keycard about.

"Sorry, man, she's not answering," Pete said smugly and indicated that I should leave as he placed his hand on his holster.

"Try her again," I said as I pulled my own phone out to

call her. It went straight to voicemail. Crap, she was probably already in bed asleep.

"It's late. I think maybe you should come back tomorrow," Pete said as he replaced the phone.

No, I hadn't come all of this way to just give up and go home. I scanned around the lobby and caught sight of the stairs. I was in excellent shape from my years at the gym. Pete looked like he could bench press me and Rex and probably Lachlan as well, but I was nippy. I was sure I could outrun him.

"Yeah, okay," I said nonchalantly, acting like I was giving up.

Pete relaxed a bit and sat back down. That was when I made my move. I shot off towards the door to the stairs at a full sprint, bursting through as I heard Pete yell, "Hey! Hey! Get back here!"

I hit the stairs at a dead run and took them two at a time. Pete was hot on my heels, but I was quicker. I ran up six flights before I surged through the door and ran to the elevator. I stabbed the button impatiently.

The doors finally slid open.

I jumped inside and pushed the button for the top floor, willing the doors to close. They slid shut and I relaxed a bit, catching my breath. The doors opened to the top floor all too soon and I leapt out and shouted straight away, "Cassie! Cassie! It's Alex, open up!" I battered on her door, thankful that she had no neighbors on this floor. "Cassie!"

"Alex?" she asked as she opened the door in surprise. "What on Earth are you doing here?"

"Just let me in," I said breathlessly as Pete came storming out of the second elevator, his gun leveled at my head.

"Don't move, you bastard," Pete growled as he stepped closer.

Cassie's eyes went wide as she held her hands up at the sight of the gun. I did the same, but thankfully Cassie recovered quickly and said, "Pete. It's okay. I know him. He's a friend."

"A friend? How do I know you aren't being coerced into saying that?" Pete asked suspiciously.

I had to give the man some credit. He took his job seriously.

"I promise I am fine, Pete," Cassie said as she carefully lowered her hands and seductively ran them down her body. Pete's eyes went straight to her magnificent cleavage, which was very apparent in the white, satin nightgown that she wore under a flimsy white robe. She looked just like the angel that Rex had called her. I was drooling at the sight of her. "Thank you so much for your concern, but you can go back to your post."

"You sure?" he asked again, still not lowering his weapon from my head. "The boss will have my head if anything happens to you."

Wow, that's dedication, I thought as I waited for this to be over. Man, twice in two days. Up to that point, I had never been held at gunpoint before and it was every bit as terrifying as I thought it would be. But I knew without a doubt I would throw myself in front of a bullet to save Cassie if I needed to.

"The boss is here," I heard Rex say from behind me.

I turned to look at him, trying not to look as terrified as I felt.

"You can let him in," he added, with a look at me that I couldn't quite place.

Pete finally lowered his weapon and holstered it. "Don't hesitate to call me if you need me," he said with a killer glare at me.

Cassie gave Rex an exasperated look but nodded as she pulled me inside and closed the door.

I breathed a sigh of relief as Cassie regarded me. "Alex, what are you doing here at this hour bothering the security?"

I glanced at Rex. "Does he know?" I asked quietly.

Cassie looked over at her lover with a soft smile. "Yes, he knows."

"And?" I asked Rex boldly, standing up straight.

"Cassie wants you here. That's good enough for me," he said shortly and then left us alone.

"And Lachlan?" I asked.

"I know he came to speak to you. He is fine," she said.

"Then, I am here for you, Cassie," I said as I took her hands. "I am not letting you get away because of my issues. I know you love me, and I love you. I have just been chased by an armed and very dedicated security guard to get to your tower and I am not leaving until you say you will be mine."

I hear a throat being cleared from the sitting room.

"Ours," I amended with a smile.

"You came all of this way, at this time of night..."

"I want you, Cassie. I am not going to leave you ever again. I promise you," I said. "Just tell me what I want to hear, and I will leave you to go back to bed."

Cassie shook her head and my heart sank, but then started to pound as she said, "I'm not going back to bed, not alone. I want you too, Alex. I also promise never to run out on you. I do love you. It means the world to me that you are willing to do this for me. I know, and appreciate, the strength that it has taken for you to come here tonight. Thank you."

"I want to be with you, however that might be," I replied. I swooped down on her mouth, gathering her to me as I kissed her gently. She ran her hands up my back and I broke off our kiss just long enough to pick her up and cradle her in my arms.

"Are you sure you want to do this?" she asked me as I carried her to the bedroom.

"Yes," I said without hesitation. I was surprised that I really meant it. I had no nervousness, no jealousy, just love for the woman in my arms.

I laid her gently on the bed, where Rex was already waiting.

Naked.

I blinked a couple of times but took a deep breath. I was here and I was doing this. If my love for Cassie wasn't enough, there was absolutely no way my ego would allow me to bail in front of the other two men now. I would never be able to face myself in the mirror if I did. That's what got me to remove my shirt. I was glad that I had a hard body. Nowhere near what Rex looked like, but I knew Cassie appreciated my six-pack. I looked over my shoulder as I sensed I was being stared at. Lachlan had joined us, also shirtless, but still in his sweats. I raked my gaze over him, to his absolute delight, taking in the fact that he was as well-built as Rex. I swallowed and my confidence wavered slightly. That was, until Cassie slid her slinky nightgown off and then all I could focus on were the daisy chains.

"Fuck," I breathed out, unable to help myself.

Lachlan chuckled at me. "Isn't she beautiful," he whispered, moving over to the bed and shedding his sweats.

I was the only one still dressed and it was becoming a bit awkward. I hastily got rid of my jeans and boxers and climbed onto the bed so that I wasn't standing around like an idiot.

Lachlan gave me a lingering look. The desire burned in his eyes, so I was glad when he turned them back to Cassie and started to kiss her.

I felt a pang. A huge one, but I pushed it aside. This is what she wanted. And I wanted her. It really did just boil down to that in the end.

I waited as Rex reached for her. He molded himself to her back, his legs on either side of her as he pinched her nipples. Hard. Her muffled yelp made me shiver, and not in a bad way. Lachlan released her mouth and licked her all the way down her chin, her neck, in between her breasts, down her stomach and to her pussy, before he delved his tongue straight into her. I took in sharp breath as she moaned. The lust at seeing her so turned on, shot through me. I knew I could do this.

I leaned over and took her nipple in my mouth, circling the daisy chain with my tongue before I tried my hand at a bit of this pain thing. I took her nipple in between my teeth and bit down gently. She gasped and ran her hand into my hair.

"Yes," she cried out. "Harder."

It was unclear which one of us she was talking to, but it didn't matter. I bit harder, Rex pinched her harder and Lachlan fucked her harder with his tongue. She was writhing in ecstasy and then she shuddered as she came.

Lachlan removed his mouth from her and grabbed my hand, shoving it in between her legs before he let me go. I touched her softly at first, but then I thrust my fingers into her. She was dripping wet and it turned me on even more. I was rock-hard, as were Rex and Lachlan. I nearly choked on my spit when I saw Lachlan reach for Rex and circle his cock. Rex stiffened, but he allowed the touch. I marveled at it. It was so new to me, but I didn't recoil from it as I thought I would. I wanted to see it. I started to breath heavily as Lachlan took Rex in his mouth, sucking on him fiercely as Cassie ran her hands over Lachlan's dick. She jerked him off as I finger-fucked her, and then Rex came, grunting loudly as he thrust into Lachlan's mouth. He swallowed it all.

I knew I was staring, but it wasn't in disgust. No, in fact I was so aroused by it. I didn't want either of them to touch me, but I was pretty okay with watching them touch each other.

~Rex~

I SQUEEZED my eyes tighter as I finished my orgasm. I don't know what I felt. But it wasn't shame. I knew that Lachlan cared about me and I could hear Cassie's heavy breathing, knowing she was turned on by watching us. I opened my eyes to find that Alex was also looking at us. He was still fingering Cassie to the point where she was ready to come from his attention, but his eyes were on me. And they were filled with desire as Lachlan pressed his lips to mine. He swept his tongue against mine, forcing me to taste myself. I gripped the back of his head, sinking into the kiss, reveling in the fact that I was turned on by someone other than Cassie. I pulled away, shoving Lachlan back to the bed. I took him in my mouth hesitantly. I had never done this before, but it felt right, and I wanted to see what it was like. I wanted to see how good I could make him feel, as he had to me. I sucked on him. Hard. Grazing my teeth down his length as he moaned in ecstasy. I cupped his balls and rolled them around in my hand.

"Fuck, yes," he cried out, but then pushed me away.

I knew it was because he wanted to come inside Cassie, so I wasn't offended. He was giving me a look of such love that it made me choke up slightly.

I cast my glance back over to Alex. He was still staring at us, his lips parted, his breathing heavy. I had been concerned about his attitude going into this. I was willing to accept him when Cassie asked me to, even more so when I figured out who he was. It felt like it was meant to be. That we had all ended up here in this place because it was where we were supposed to be. But it seemed that he was here to please Cassie, just as Lachlan and I were. She was the only thing that mattered. Any feelings that we had that weren't about her, were just a bonus as far as I was concerned. I had never cared about anyone except Cassandra and I had never had anyone care about me until I met her. And not only did I know that she loved me, I knew that Lachlan did too. It made me feel like I could be normal again. That I didn't have to feel evil and wrong and like I was a monster. I also knew that I felt more than gratitude towards Alex. I didn't know him, but I thought we could eventually have something akin to love between us. Even if it was just as friends.

I found Cassie's eyes, they were alight with lust and it turned me on in ways that I could only imagine.

"We have indulged ourselves for long enough," I murmured. "This is Cassie's time."

She giggled. "I don't mind," she said before she lowered

her mouth to Lachlan, licking down his entire length before she took him in her mouth. She spread her legs wide in invitation to Alex, who didn't hesitate to slide in between them. He thrust into her and she cried out. I dragged her away from Lachlan as I just had to kiss her. Kissing her was like nothing else in this world. She moaned into my mouth as Alex pounded into her. He made her come in violent shudders. She pulled away and cried out, pushing her breasts together with her hands so she could play with her nipples.

"Fuck," Lachlan said and leaned over her, flicking them with his tongue, light touches that drove her wild. "Alex."

Alex looked up, intent on fucking Cassie to another orgasm.

Lachlan trailed a finger in between her pushed up mounds.

"Oh yes," Cassie moaned. "Please."

Alex pulled out of her as she begged him to tit-fuck her. He slid his dick in between her breasts with a groan of pure lust.

"Fuck, Cassie," he muttered as he pumped and pumped.

I was mesmerized. I wanted to see him come all over her face. So did she. I knew her. I knew it aroused her.

I waited, holding my breath as I laced my fingers through hers. Lachlan had taken over pushing her breasts together, his mouth so close. He flicked his tongue out, touching Alex's cock with the tip. Alex grunted in surprise, but it was too late. He was pumping harder and with a groan of satisfaction, he came, spurting out over Cassie's chest and into, not only *her* open mouth, but Lachlan's as well.

Alex's eyes went wide with horror, but when he looked

down at Cassie, and saw her extreme pleasure at the small act, he breathed in and smiled. "Fuck, Cassie," he said again. "You are the sexiest thing I have ever seen."

He collapsed on the bed next to her and then it was Lachlan's turn. But he didn't want to go where anyone else had yet.

~Cassie~

I WAS IN HEAVEN. If I had thought it was amazing to be loved by Rex and Lachlan, adding Alex into it had made it absolutely perfect.

I could still taste his cum in my mouth as Lachlan positioned me on my hands and knees. I gasped as he licked around my rear hole. I'd had anal sex before, but only once. I knew he'd wanted this to be a double penetration scenario, but it wasn't going to happen this time. At least not the way he wanted it. He lubed me up with his saliva, circling my hole in a luscious movement that sent rockets of desire shooting through me. My toes were tingling with the antici-pation. He pressed his cock at my entrance and pushed gently. I gasped as he eased his way into me. I was focused on Lachlan, so I started slightly when I felt Rex's fingers pushing into my pussy.

"Ooo," I breathed out. "Aah!"

Alex had placed his fingers on my clit and was circling it enticingly as Rex pulsed in and out of my pussy and Lach-lan, now all the way inside my ass, started to thrust.

"Oh, Cassie," Lachlan groaned. "I love you."

"I love you," I murmured. It was the first time I had told him. He gripped my hips tighter and pounded into me. "I love all of you," I screamed as an orgasm so fierce ripped through me from their attentions. Wave after wave of pleasure washed over me as I was thoroughly loved from every angle. Rex kissed my lips as Alex nipped at my shoulder.

Lachlan slammed into me, rocking me forward, but then he pulled out and shoved lower down, straight into my dripping wet pussy, while Rex's fingers were still inside me.

"Oh, Jesus!" I cried, feeling them both inside me.

"Alex," Rex murmured.

I heard Alex rasp; his breathing heavy as he also inserted his fingers into me. Another climax peaked, making me scream out in pure ecstasy. I had never felt an orgasm so intense before and it made it happen again. I was sweating with the effort of staying on my hands and knees, clenching around them again before Lachlan let go, shooting his load into me, all over Rex and Alex's fingers.

He pulled out of me and I crumpled to the bed completely worn out. Fuck, if it was going to be like this every night, I would have to give up working. I would be way too tired and blissed out to move.

"You get fifteen minutes," Rex said. "Then I am going to fuck you so hard, you will scream."

I groaned with pleasure. "Yes, please," I exclaimed to his delight.

I caught Alex's eye and he smiled at me. He took my hand and linked our fingers. Then he turned to Rex and said, "Blindfold her. I want to see it."

The rush of love that I had for him in that moment, made me break out into a happy smile.

"Mm," Lachlan murmured. "I want to see it too."

I laid back and rested for a few minutes as I was gently kissed, sucked and licked by all three of my men until not only was I ready to go again, but so were they.

I was the luckiest woman on the planet.

THIRTY-ONE

~Cassie~

"Morning," Alex said as I woke up and stretched. I was in a tangle with Rex on one side of me, Lachlan on the other and Alex, already up, handing me a cup of coffee.

I gave him a brilliant smile and said, "Hi. I was so worried that when I woke up, this would have just been a dream."

"Not a chance," he said and returned my smile. "I have one question."

"What's that?" I asked taking a sip.

"Are you my girlfriend again?"

I chuckled, but before I could say anything, Lachlan piped up. "She is, but she is also mine and Rex's."

"I can live with that," he said softly, sitting back down and taking my foot to massage gently.

"Mm, me too," I said.

"Good," Alex replied. "Because this time, you are going to be my real, not-so-secret girlfriend."

I sighed at him as he brought up the unpleasant topic I had been pushing aside since he stormed my castle to tell me he wanted me. "Alex, we still work together," I ventured, not really sure how to get around this problem.

"Not for much longer," he said cryptically.

I propped myself up on my elbows, disturbing Rex as I did so. "What do you mean by that?"

"I mean, Ms. Bellingham, that I hereby offer you my resignation, effective immediately," Alex stated with as much dignity as he could while naked in my bed as I flashed my tits at him.

"What?" I shrieked at him. "You can't resign, I just promoted you."

"I know, but you have a handful of people you can replace the position with. I only have the one you and you cannot be replaced," he said with a slight smile

I melted into a gooey puddle at his words.

"He has a way with words, this one," Lachlan said, giving him a shrewd look with one open brown eye. "I like him."

"I like you too," Alex said lightly.

Lachlan's other eye opened as he grinned. He reached out and played with my nipples as if it was the most natural thing in the world. Heat flared within me and I moaned. I leaned back to let Alex's hands wander up my legs and flit lightly across my pussy. I was sore down there and aching in every part of my body, but I didn't care. It was perfect.

"But what will you do?" I asked, concerned.

"I already have another job," he said, avoiding my eyes.

"Oh?" I asked tartly. "Where, pray tell?"

"Londis Corp. They offered it to me a week ago, I was working up the nerve to tell you."

"A week ago?" I asked, confused. "When did you start looking?" I added suspiciously.

"Right after our first night together," he replied. "I knew that I needed every part of you and to do that I had to leave. And then I wanted to leave after we, you know...I couldn't stand being in the same building as you and not having you."

"Are you sure this is what you want?" I asked. I couldn't let him give up his job for me.

"I want *you*," he said simply.

"It's not fair," Rex mumbled into my shoulder.

"What isn't?" I asked him in surprise.

"He gets to make this grand fucking gesture. It's not fair."

Lachlan snorted in amusement. "It is pretty hot. We are going to have to up our game, Angelwings."

Rex sat up suddenly at the nickname. I stifled my laugh. It was Lachlan's way. He found a nickname for everyone and it stuck whether you liked it or not. Sweetcheeks wasn't the nice endearment you'd think it was. It was given to me after I sat in bubblegum on a field trip to the Tower of London and wandered all around the city with it stuck to my ass.

"I like it," I decided. "It is very fitting."

Lachlan nodded his approval at my agreement. "And you..." He gave Alex a thoughtful look. "Give me time, stud."

Alex chuckled. "Please, nothing embarrassing," he begged.

"We'll see," Lachlan commented and then fell promptly back to sleep.

"I wish I could sleep like him," Rex said as he snuggled into me and kissed my shoulder.

"Me too," I said. "You are a nightmare insomniac." I gave him a pointed look. I expected him to start opening up to me, the sooner the better.

He shrugged, exchanging a look with Alex that made me extremely curious. Seems everyone knew something about this man, except me.

I knew he would tell me in his own time. I just hoped he wasn't going to put it off indefinitely. We needed to trust each other if this was going to work, and I *really* wanted it to work.

THIRTY-TWO

One Year Later

~Lachlan~

"Hey," Cassie murmured seductively as soon as Alex stepped in the penthouse. We were sitting on the sofa watching TV, holding hands and enjoying a private moment, just the two of us.

"Hey, yourself," he said. "How are two of my favorite people?" He leaned down to kiss her and she deepened it momentarily. Then he turned to me and gave me that smile that had me growing hard before he leaned over and brushed his lips against mine.

I didn't take it further. He was slowly coming around, but I wasn't going to rush him. What he gave me was genuine and came from his heart. That was good enough for me. For now.

"Where's the third?" he asked, looking around.

"Rex had a job come up," Cassie said.

At her choice of words, I exchanged a look with Alex, which he returned. We had a secret from Cassie. The one and only. We had never told Cassie what Rex used to do. He had gone legit now, working in I.T. as his cover stated. Mostly I forgot about it, but when things like that popped up, it reminded me of his former life. He had eventually opened up about it one night when Cassie was working late. Alex and I had been there for him, and the whole sordid lot came out. I was more than surprised that he and Alex had a history, and Alex was shocked as fuck when he heard about the hitman for hire part of the story. But, true to his word, he had kept the secret. I trusted him with my life. I knew Rex did too, and it was definitely reciprocated. We were in this together.

"He should be back soon though," she said, looking at the clock.

As if on cue, he walked out of the elevator and gave us a curious look. "What?" he asked.

"I'm glad you are here," Cassie said, jumping up and going over to grab his hand. He leaned down to kiss her and let her drag him to the sofa. "I have something to tell all of you."

I sat up, curious. I knew something was up with her. She was jumpy and distracted.

"Everything okay?" Alex asked, before I could.

She nodded cautiously. "I think so."

"Whatever it is, you can tell us," Rex said, pushing her down gently and sitting next to her, gripping her hand tightly. Alex perched on the coffee table, putting his hand on her knee as I grabbed her other hand.

"I hope so," she said and looked at each of us in turn. "I want you to know that I will do whatever we decide here, it has to be one hundred percent agreed as I don't want anyone feeling resentment or worry or anything else negative about this."

"Have you found someone else?" Rex asked quietly, the only one of us prepared to say it out loud as we were all thinking it.

"What?" she asked. "No, don't be silly. It's nothing like that."

We all breathed out in relief.

She took in a deep breath. "I'm pregnant," she blurted out.

"What?" the three of us asked in unison as stunned as each other.

She bit her lip, suddenly looking nervous.

"I suppose it is a stupid question to ask whose it is?" I asked sardonically.

"Just a bit," she replied, rolling her eyes at me. "I don't care whose it is. It is ours. All of ours. But we need to decide what to do."

"What does that mean?" Alex asked, giving her a slightly angry look. "You can't honestly be thinking about... not having it," he finished up as I glared at him.

"What do *you* want to do?" I asked her, squeezing her hand.

"I want it," she said simply. "It was created out of love; we are in a position to have this child and love it completely. But we all need to agree," she reiterated.

"I want it," Rex blurted out. "I don't care if it isn't mine."

"Same," I said, and we all looked at Alex.

"Obviously," he huffed. "Although, are we going to find out?"

I felt Cassie relax as we all got on the same page about keeping the child.

"No," I said.

Cassie shook her head.

"No," Rex agreed, and Alex nodded in agreement.

"There, that wasn't so hard now was it," I crooned to her.

"No," she laughed nervously. "I was petrified one of you would tell me to get rid of it."

"Never," Rex growled.

"It will come out looking like...someone," Alex said, "Just saying," he added as I gave him a swat round the back of the head. "I mean we all look very different. What then?"

"We revisit," Cassie suggested.

I nodded, but I didn't really care. I would love any child that Cassie had whether it was my own or not. "It doesn't matter. This child will want for nothing. It has four parents who will adore him or her. We will make sure that this child never has to grow up wondering why it wasn't loved."

Cassie's eyes filled with tears. "I love you all so much." She wept openly and we held her tenderly. "We will have to tell my grandparents soon. I don't know how they will take it."

"They will be fine. If they could accept all of us shacking up together, then this will be nothing. Besides, Ruby will be over the moon to have a great-grandchild," I reassured her. I knew she didn't give a flying fuck about her parents. I don't think she even bothered to tell them about us herself, leaving them to find out via the grapevine. I didn't give a shit. Ruby and William I respected but Damien and Suzanne could go and get fucked.

"Can we still..." Alex asked wickedly, tilting his head towards the playroom.

"Don't be a caveman," Rex growled at him. "She needs to be treated with care."

Cassie laughed with delight. Alex had come out of his shell enormously these last few months. He enjoyed his naughty side and I really enjoyed watching him. "Of course," she said, "Just go easy on me."

"Always," Alex replied, giving her a deep kiss.

It aroused me to see her kissed like that. I pulled her onto my lap, pushing her dress up her hips. She wasn't wearing any panties which was to our liking. I shuffled underneath her to get myself free, pushing my fingers into her. I lubed up and stuck my wet fingers into her ass. She squirmed and tilted herself back to get more comfortable. Alex pulled his cock from his pants. He stroked his length, getting it as hard for her as he could. I removed my fingers and placed my cock at her puckered hole. I gave a gentle thrust and she cried out softly. I settled her, letting Rex unbutton her dress and peel it off her, exposing her perfect tits to us. I loved it when she didn't wear a bra, choosing to encase her magnificent rack in a tight dress instead. Alex stripped off the rest of his suit and leaned over, placing one knee on the sofa next to me. He let me stroke him a couple of times before he grabbed hold of himself and inserted his cock into Cassie's pussy slowly.

"Oh, fuck, yes," she cried out as we impaled her from both ends.

Rex attached himself to her nipple, grinding down on her with his teeth. She yelped and he eased up a bit, sucking gently and then pulling back to lick her.

Alex came quickly, he always did when we took her this way. It was a massive turn on for him. I held off with great difficulty. I loved watching him come. It was intense and made my heart beat faster. He pulled out as the first wave of her orgasm hit her, allowing Rex entry as her pussy twitched and got wetter as she folded around him. He closed his eyes and jerked his hips. Sliding in and out of her with ease. It was too much for me. I shot my load into her ass with a guttural moan that made her whimper with need. Rex withdrew and pulled her up, turning her around so that he could fuck her in her ass. I shoved my fingers up into her roughly, knowing it would be the last time for a while that she let us use her like this. Alex's fingers joined mine to bring her to an earth-shattering orgasm that rocked all of our worlds. Rex came quickly after that and then he picked her up and carried her to our bedroom. He laid her down gently and kissed her stomach.

"I'm happy," he whispered to her. "You have made me so happy. I love you."

I climbed onto the bed next to her and held her close to me, as Alex did the same. We lay like that for the rest of the night. Just being with each other. Letting each other know that we loved them with small gestures and gentle touches, light kisses and intense lovemaking.

~Cassie~

ONE MONTH TO THE DAY, after I told my men that I was pregnant, I stood calming my nerves. We had scrambled to get this done in four short weeks because I did not want to walk down the proverbial aisle, looking like a whale. I was already three months pregnant. I waited, keeping my secret from them for nearly a month before I told them. I needed to be absolutely certain that what I was about to tell them was the truth. I was glad that they'd accepted it so readily. I had been so nervous about telling them. It wasn't part of the plan. I was being responsible, of course I was. But I could tell you exactly when it happened. A sickness bug had swept through the office like wildfire and I had thrown up for two straight days. I felt and looked like death warmed over, so as soon as I felt better, I took all three of my men in quick succession. So, it really was anyone's guess who the baby belonged to. But I didn't care. And neither did they. Alex was right in saying that one day we would see who the child favored in looks, but until that day, we were happy to leave it. None of us would love it any less and the two who weren't the biological father wouldn't hold it against the father or the child. We would love it completely.

One thing I was certain of though, was that we had to make this official. Well, as official as we could get under our set of circumstances. Which had led us here, to this beautiful, end-of-summer day in Central Park.

"Are you ready for this, girl?" Granddaddy asked me.

"Yes," I replied with a bright smile, so happy that he was here with me.

Our ceremony was small. Only the four of us, my grandparents, Uncle Teddy and Lachlan's parents had been invited. No one else mattered. Rex had finally told me that his mother was dead, and I already knew Alex would never speak to his mother again. I still couldn't believe that Rex and Alex had a history that went back so many years. It proved to me that we were connected long before any of us we aware of it and that, to me, meant it was fate.

I took in a deep breath and took Granddaddy's arm. I was about to tie myself to my three men in an old Pagan Handfast ritual. So, it wasn't the traditional church wedding Grandmother had always dreamed of for me, but our relationship was far from traditional.

"Thank you for doing this," I whispered to him.

"Of course, child," he said gruffly. "You are a good girl, Cassandra. You have made me so very proud of you."

His simple sentence made tears spring to my eyes. It meant more to me than I could ever say.

"Agh," he grumbled. "If you start that, then your grandmother will start, and I am too old to deal with the crying thing."

I giggled. It was the right thing to say. My eyes dried and we started the short walk towards the makeshift altar.

My men stared at me, in my green dress that floated around my ankles in the soft breeze, with such love I nearly choked up.

"You're up, Suits," Lachlan murmured, his face a mask of emotion.

When I reached them, standing under the beautiful white gazebo, Alex popped a daisy chain crown on top of my head. It made me laugh with delight. "Perfect," I told him.

He took my arm from my grandfather's and turned towards the woman conducting the ceremony.

The only way we could agree on how to do this was to go alphabetically. I only had two hands and three men, so we decided to do it individually. It didn't mean anything. We were all equal, but someone had to go first.

———

THIRTY MINUTES LATER, I was a married woman, three times over. I'd decided to keep my Bellingham name, as would my baby. It was the fairest way, and one that we all agreed on. As I turned and looked at the small gathering, clapping and celebrating our love, I caught the interested gazes of the passers-by. Some puzzled, some envious, but mostly judgmental. I didn't give a shit. The only people whose opinions mattered to me where here, supporting us on our special day. I was the proudest woman on the planet to have three such wonderful, gorgeous, kind men love me as much as they did. I would make sure that they knew how much I loved them, every day for the rest of our lives.

As I turned back to my husbands, a chill slid down my spine. I felt like I was being undressed by someone's eyes and it gave me the creeps. All of a sudden, I wanted to leave this happy place and return to the sanctuary of my home with my new husbands by my side.

The End

Keep Reading! The 2nd Enchained Hearts Book: Lives Entangled is available now.

Join my Facebook Reader Group for more info on my latest books and backlist: Forever Eve's Reader Group

Join my newsletter for exclusive news,

giveaways and competitions: http://
eepurl.com/gZNCdL

ABOUT THE AUTHOR

Eve is a British novelist with a specialty for paranormal romance, with strong female leads, causing her to develop a Reverse Harem Fantasy series, several years ago: The Forever Series.

She lives in the UK, with her husband and five kids, so finding the time to write is short, but definitely sweet. She currently has two on-going series, with a number of spin-offs in the making. Eve hopes to release some new and exciting projects in the next couple of years, so stay tuned!

Start Eve's Reverse Harem Fantasy Series, with the first two books in the Forever Series as a double edition!

Newsletter Sign up for exclusive content and giveaways: http://eepurl.com/bxilBT

Facebook Reader Group: https://www.face-book.com/groups/ForeverEves

Facebook: http://facebook.com/evenewtonforever

Twitter: https://twitter.com/AuthorEve

Website: https://evenewton.com/

ALSO BY EVE NEWTON

Find a comprehensive list of Eve's books here:

https://evenewton.com/books-by-eve

Printed in Great Britain
by Amazon

75374539R00137